Mara whipped about, her heart racing like a speeding deer.

A bare-chested Native American, hair loose to his shoulders, emerged from the semidarkness. Though he was tall and handsome, his shadowed expression frightened her.

"You," he growled. "Come to me."

Mara shrank back. Yet an inexplicable longing battled fear. Her lips parted, but she could not speak.

The stranger—yet somehow not a stranger—moved toward her, pulling her tightly against his body. He raked his hands over her as if he owned her, as if he were memorizing every inch of flesh. And then he savaged her mouth....

Suddenly Mara awoke sobbing, heart pounding. Was she going mad? She mourned for a virtual stranger... for the achingly familiar emotions he stirred in her.

What power did this man hold over her?

Dear Reader,

One of our veteran Shadows authors is back this month, and she's written exactly the kind of eerily romantic book you've come to expect from this line.

Jeanne Rose returns with *Heart of Dreams,* in which dreams are far more than fantasies created by our sleeping minds to resolve waking issues. These dreams are real, even terrifying. And sometimes very, very sensual.

I hope you enjoy our offering this month, and that you'll come back next month, ready for another walk on the dark side of love with Silhouette Shadows.

Yours,

Leslie Wainger
Senior Editor and Editorial Coordinator

Please address questions and book requests to:
Silhouette Reader Service
U.S.: 3010 Walden Ave., P.O. Box 1325, Buffalo, NY 14269
Canadian: P.O. Box 609, Fort Erie, Ont. L2A 5X3

JEANNE ROSE

Heart of
DREAMS

SILHOUETTE® Shadows™

Published by Silhouette Books
America's Publisher of Contemporary Romance

Thanks to Cheryl and Rick for turning us on to Santa Fe,
and
thanks to John Milton Wilson

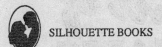 SILHOUETTE BOOKS

ISBN 0-373-27055-0

HEART OF DREAMS

Copyright © 1995 by Patricia Pinianski & Linda Sweeney

Books by Jeanne Rose

Silhouette Shadows

The Prince of Air and Darkness #26
Heart of Dreams #55

Silhouette Romance

Believing in Angels #913
Love on the Run #1027

JEANNE ROSE

is the newest pseudonym of Patricia Pinianski and Linda Sweeney. The Chicagoans have been a team since 1982, when they met in a writing class. Now Linda teaches writing at two suburban community colleges and works for *Writer's Digest*, while Patricia makes writing her full-time focus. Patricia and Linda are happy they can combine their fascination with the mysterious and magical with their belief in the triumph of love. Patricia and Linda are also known as Lynn Patrick, and Patricia writes as Patricia Rosemoor.

The authors wish it to be known that the Native American beliefs in this book are fictitious and have been extrapolated from mythology books and visits to New Mexican reservations. The Pueblo Rebellion actually happened, but there is no clan called the Kisi among Pueblo Indians.

PROLOGUE

An invasion of light made her stir and squeeze her lids tight. She turned her head to the side to deny the light's power, but it followed as if it were inside her skull... insistent... compelling.

Begrudgingly giving up the fight, she opened her eyes. The brilliance of the morning almost blinded her, made her shrink back into herself and pull her cover over her head. A moment passed before she realized what she had seen. Confusion gripped her and she forced herself to peek out from her striped covering.

This was not possible.

She lay on the earthen floor of a large canyon. Stones bit into her back and a howling wind swept over her body, yet she hardly felt either, as if earth and elements were figments of her imagination. An eerie foreboding made her want to swallow and take a deep breath. Her throat was too parched; her tongue clung to the roof of her dry mouth. She could hardly speak.

"Good Lord, where am I?"

More important, how had she gotten there when she'd fallen asleep in a bed?

A rush of adrenaline sluiced through her as she jumped to her feet. Her head went light and her pulse pounded so hard she thought it might split her in two. The striped bed sheet was the only barrier between her and the environment. Nude beneath the thin mate-

rial, she wrapped the sheet more tightly around her like a huge enveloping cape and peered out of the narrow slit.

In the distance, the sun rose over a mountaintop, blazing color into the dry earth as if with a fiery paintbrush. Closer by were tangles of chamisa and stark-looking juniper bushes. And midway between the majestic blue peaks and the crimson earth on which she stood, a single thin finger of green meadow pointed to ancient rock formations—deep red cliffs balancing huge boulders.

She tried not to panic.

"Hello!" she shouted. "Is anyone there?"

The words sang along the cliffs where they mutated and returned as unearthly whispers that surrounded her and brushed her insides with an unsettling certainty. Her stomach knotted with panic as the silence grew.

No answer.

She was alone.

Frightened, she drew the sheet closer against the stiff wind that threatened to deprive her of her only protection. The material fluttered in sharp bursts as the air caught and plucked at it like a mischievous child. Her fingers bunched and tightened until they ached.

She scanned the area.

Desolate...forbidding...ghostly...rough-cut rocks weathered and wrinkled, successive layers striated in varying shades of red-brown... the ends of the earth... unfit for human habitation.

But wait. A tiny figure shimmered in the distance, atop a flat, bloodred mesa.

Before she even thought to move, her legs impelled her forward. The hard-packed earth and stones grazed her bare feet, the contact featherlike. Around her, translucent canyon walls zoomed by faster and faster until they were nothing more than a blur. Her heavy breath melded with the wind and resonated through her head. The tiny figure multiplied in size until she could identify a woman sitting cross-legged, face passive as if closed in sleep, wild black hair whipping out around a brightly colored torso. And yet the woman seemed somehow unreal.

Above, the sky shifted. Gray and purple clouds rolled in, swallowing the sun. A flash of lightning struck rock behind the apparition, whose bronzed features were clearly Native American and whose dark eyes opened wide, reflecting horror. A crash of thunder rang out.

"Who are you?" the Indian woman shouted, her hollow voice riding on the wind.

Who...?

The question paralyzed her, and yet, somehow, she had already made her way to the top of the mesa. Through the slit in her protective cloak of a sheet, she stared at the woman who seemed real and yet not. Her chest heaved and she tried to speak—to answer—but no words would come.

Hair flying, features distorted, the Indian rushed forward, hands raised in a gesture of self-protection. "Who are you? What is your name?"

She moved her mouth but made no sound.

She couldn't speak, couldn't answer.

She did not know.

Lightning split both sky and earth. The wind howled and tried to rip the sheet from her clawed fingers. The woman screeched at her, demanding her name over and over. A sudden terror made her back away from the threatening apparition, knowing her name would save her... yet having no answer.

Panicked, she turned to run from the banshee, only to be enveloped by a waiting void....

CHAPTER ONE

"Aah!" Mara Fitzgerald flew upward in bed, her limbs tangled in the sheet, her skin covered in a cold sweat. Sunlight spilled into the room. Her heartbeat was frenzied. Another bizarre nightmare, different than the others.

Worse.

Not knowing her own name made her feel as if she were losing her identity.

She clutched the sheet around her and vaulted out of bed as if leaving the scene of her dream would dissipate the fear that was making her pulse thud in jagged strokes. But the eerie images wouldn't be vanquished. The setting of the nightmare was familiar somehow....

Her knees scarcely supporting her, Mara backed out of the bedroom and into the shadows of the hallway. Cool adobe met her bare shoulders, and she tilted her head back against the wall. She forced herself to relax, to breathe normally. Her mouth and throat were dry, as in the dream.

Her eyes adjusting to the dimness, Mara became aware of the painting on the opposite wall. Good Lord, that was it. Frantic to get a better look, she switched on the track lighting.

Lightning Over Red Mesa, painted by Lucas Naha. The piece she'd bought years before while still working in the San Francisco gallery. Though small, the painting and its haunting beauty cast a powerful spell. That's why she'd hung it here in the narrow hall where she could admire it at will, rather than in a room where she couldn't avoid it.

Mara took in every detail of the painting, from the distant mountains shrouded in gray-and-purple clouds to the desolate canyon floor. Her eyes were drawn to the streak of lightning that connected the sky to the broad red mesa upon which sat a tiny, barely discernable figure.

Relief flowed through her. This nightmare, at least, had an explanation. Lucas Naha had been making her new job as manager of Sol Goldstein's Santa Fe gallery difficult. In turn, the problem with the artist had produced her anxiety-ridden dream.

Only one thing still bothered her....

Why hadn't she known who she was?

Fear clutched Isabel Joshevama's throat as she came out of her self-induced trance. Her sightless eyes opened to a wall of light and shadow, but she could still see her surroundings as vividly as she had viewed them for seven decades before losing her sight. Every stone, every crevice, every shade of red of this mesa was burned into her memory.

She saw every detail when she went dreamseeking. She wasn't blind in her visions.

Not any more than she was oblivious to danger.

For now the unknown had invaded, menaced, was perhaps endangering what remained of this fragile lifetime. She stirred, fully aware of her own mortality.

"You are with me?" asked her companion.

Isabel reached out and grabbed Rebecca Harvier's arm. "I am no longer safe."

"What did you see?"

"A stranger swathed in striped material."

"This stranger threatened you?"

"I asked for a name, but the specter was clever and would not answer. It deliberately hid from me, covered itself from head to foot so I could not see its face. Nor even make out its sex." She tightened her hold on the woman who had become her eyes in her earthbound world. "I demanded that it answer me." No small request since Isabel possessed all the power of a *finished person,* a wisewoman of the pueblo. "But it stayed silent, backed away, then disappeared." She took a deep breath. "Rebecca, someone has entered my dreaming place, someone with enough power to withstand me."

"An ancient one?"

"Surely not, or the spirit would have identified itself."

"Charlie Mahooty?" Rebecca whispered, sounding horrified.

A chill shot through Isabel at the mention of a power monger who meant their people ill. For once, she could not answer.

Mara entered the small courtyard of Aspen Plaza, named for the old tree at its heart. A warm summer breeze swirled her brown hair around her shoulders as it gave voice to the aspen's shimmering foliage. The whisper of wind caught and fluttered the leaves' broad surfaces. She shivered, feeling as if the wind had a message meant for her alone.

A sense of something dark and frightening nudged her awareness. She felt wary and on edge—the after-effects of the dream.

She tried to chase away the unsettling feelings, tried to tell herself she'd fallen under the spell of the dancing ground of the sun, New Mexico, with all the strange beliefs of its three cultures—Anglo, Hispanic and Native American.

Mara drew herself together as she traversed the flagstone path. Back in San Francisco, while first attending art school, then working toward a graduate degree in art therapy, she'd been employed as the owner's assistant at the Sol Goldstein Gallery. Now, after working six years as an art therapist—a profession that combined art and psychology by using art materials to work with mental patients—she was back in the gallery business, this time as the new manager of Sol's Santa Fe branch.

The gallery was located on East Palace Avenue, barely a block off the main square. Aspen Plaza was part of a *trazo,* a series of Spanish-colonial buildings with interior courtyards and common walls forming a continuous facade along the street. The successful, upscale establishment filled the entire first floor of the north wing.

Mara crossed under the territorial-style portal and left the morning's warmth for the coolness of the gallery. The central room was bright and inviting with its red tile floor and small seating area around a white-washed corner kiva fireplace. Paintings and prints graced the walls, and weavings and pottery decorated small tables and several niches built into the adobe.

Strangely enough, the place was deserted. Mara was wondering where Felice Paquin, her assistant, had gone when the exotic-featured woman, whose heritage included all three cultures, suddenly shot up from behind the reception desk.

Mara jumped and gave a squeak of surprise.

"Hey, I didn't mean to scare you." Smiling, Felice tossed her dark hair from her face. "I was checking the phone connection under the desk."

Feeling foolish, Mara said, "I'm just on edge."

"Haven't shut off the hard-driving, big-city attitude, huh?"

"I guess. I had a nightmare last night."

Not like one of the terrifying dreams she'd started having as a child. The vivid chases had made her wake up screaming, had led her to invest herself in a quest for understanding, and eventually had prompted her to seek a profession that combined creative expression with psychology.

Nor had this dream been another macabre nightmare of dead bodies. Those dreams had begun invading her nights after the suicide of a mental patient she'd been treating. Guilt-ridden and devastated, she'd burned out on her job after barely a half-dozen years as an art therapist. That's when she'd gone to Sol to ask for her old gallery job back.

But this morning's dream had been frightening in its own way, and, for a moment, Mara couldn't help wondering if she was on the verge of a nervous breakdown.

She told Felice, "I dreamed I was in one of Lucas Naha's paintings."

The pretty brunette snorted. "No wonder, after all the trouble we've been having with that jerk."

Mara smiled wryly. Though she was fully aware that some artists were difficult, often because they'd traveled a rough road to success, she did get annoyed when someone got too full of himself.

Naha's work was overdue, and his nervous agent hadn't been able to hurry the man, not even with warnings of a lawsuit or the possibility of his being replaced by another artist as Goldstein's main draw. The gallery had scheduled and advertised a Lucas Naha opening to take place the following week. Now there was no assurance there'd be anything to sell.

Walking back to the storeroom together, the two women passed *Sun Dog,* a huge canvas of bigger-than-life New Mexico landscape. Distant mountains loomed over a small village above which the clouds were split by a sun dog—a spray of brilliant light that gave the illusion of drawing water and land to the sky.

A land and sky that suddenly seemed familiar, Mara realized, catching her breath as she stopped to stare.

"You've heard about the mysticism surrounding Naha's paintings, haven't you?" Felice asked.

Chills shot up Mara's spine. "Mysticism?"

Felice pointed at the tiny figure near the village, the only human in the landscape. "Many collectors believe these small beings have a life of their own. Supposedly, they move around, at times occupying different parts of the canvas."

And might they also be able to enter one's dreams? Mara wondered with another thrill.

"The Kisi tribe are called 'the cursed ones' by other Southwestern Indians," Felice went on. "And they have a reputation for sorcery like the Yaquis."

"You mean they're considered to be evil?"

"No, of course not. Sorcery can be either evil or good, depending on the purpose of the person who uses it. And the Kisi are said to be cursed by something that happened in the past."

Taking a better look at *Sun Dog,* Mara noted the little figure was in the same place it always had been. Earthy, yet otherworldly in their near-magical realism, Naha's paintings never failed to move her, though she'd be damned if she'd allow them to haunt her.

Not any more than she would let a touchy artist make her job more difficult than it was.

Frustration and anxiety had made her abandon her career as an art therapist, a profession in which she'd invested so much of herself. This job could never be so stressful as the last; she'd work things out, even if she personally had to wring a couple more paintings out of Naha.

At least a life wasn't hanging in the balance. Mara still remembered every detail of the last session she'd had with a suicidal patient—he'd wanted her to enter his dreams and rescue him from a monster. She'd told him to draw or paint the monster to get it out of his system and had assured him no one could enter someone else's dreams....

Again, the chills. Mara didn't particularly want to believe in mysticism, much less sorcery.

Lucas Naha had created imagery of such power, it had entered her subconscious, could affect her even while she slept. Mara realized how deeply she longed to meet an artist who could do that. Maybe talking to Naha could give her some insight into her terrible dreams, help her figure out what made her susceptible to them in the first place.

Once more, she played over the details of her nightmare, the Indian woman who had seemed so alive, the landscape that had seemed so familiar...

And she determined to face them while awake.

The country seventy miles northwest of Santa Fe had a vast and unspoiled air. Mara was instantly drawn to the landscape the same way she had been attracted to Naha's paintings, almost as if she had some personal connection to the place.

Which confused her. And made her apprehensive.

Or else she was scared of meeting the artist, who had a difficult, antisocial reputation. But as an art therapist in a city hospital in-patient unit, Mara had dealt with difficult administrators and demanding psychiatrists, as well as paranoid schizophrenics who thought they were messiahs destined to lead the earth into Armageddon. Surely a reclusive artist with mystical leanings and restless figures was small potatoes.

She would merely ask Naha a few questions, remind him firmly, if diplomatically, of his contract with the gallery. But, mainly, she'd assuage her curiosity and lay her own fears to rest. In the same way that patients overcame anxieties by representing them and talking about them as art, she would face the man whose imagery had played a leading role in her nightmare, recognize him for the talented if ordinary person he had to be and banish him and his paintings from any further late-night horror shows.

Feeling more confident over her impetuous decision to visit the Kisi reservation that very afternoon, Mara flicked on the car's cruise control, then sat back to survey the scenery. She seemed to be alone on the road that wound its way among stark red foothills. Beyond stood compelling blue-gray mountains, once the home of the ancient Anasazi. The cliff-dwelling Native Americans had built their villages on rocky precipices nearly a thousand years before the Spanish arrived in North America.

Like all Pueblos, the Kisi traced their roots back to the Anasazi, but since had mixed their blood with nomads like Comanches and Navajos, especially after the group had nearly been wiped out in 1691. Mara had read that a Spanish captain by the name of Francisco Castillo had been especially vicious with the Kisi, who'd managed to hold out for quite some time. The ensuing massacre was the reason other tribes said the Kisi were cursed.

A half hour later, when she drove up the thinly graveled road leading into the reservation, she saw sad proof that the Indians still weren't thriving. An old church and a cluster of small houses—mostly adobe, some of cinder block—sat among juniper bushes and scraggly trees. When she honked her horn, a scrawny dog got out of the road and ran to hide behind an abandoned-looking pickup truck nearby.

Where did Naha live? Since there didn't seem to be any names or numbers on any of the houses, she decided to ask directions at the general store. Pulling her car up in front of the one-story adobe building, Mara got out. The moment her foot touched soil, another thrill of cognition shot through her. But the sensation dissipated equally quickly. She went inside.

Two men were involved in a heated discussion at the counter, the storekeeper slim and in his thirties, the customer heavyset, greasy haired and probably a decade older.

"You haven't paid your tab, Mahooty." The storekeeper nervously pushed at his aviator glasses. "I can't let you have anything else until you clear it up."

"I want a carton of cigarettes." The heavyset man pounded his fist on the counter. "And I want it *now*."

"Hey, can't you at least make a payment? I'm operating a business here."

"I don't have to make a payment. I run this reservation."

"If I don't get paid, I'll have to close down."

With a growl, Mahooty tore a bill from his pocket. "All right, here's five bucks. Give me the cigarettes."

The storekeeper scooped up the money and fetched the carton from a shelf behind him. Grabbing his purchase, Mahooty turned to leave, his eyes narrowing on Mara as he passed her.

She approached the counter. "Could you give me directions? I'm looking for Lucas Naha."

"Hmm, Naha?" His eyes were bright and curious behind the aviators. "Are you an art collector?"

"I'm the manager at Sol Goldstein's."

Continuing to stare, the man smiled broadly and reached over the counter to shake Mara's hand. "I'm an artist myself, a sculptor. Tom Chalas. Are you looking for new talent? I'd be happy to show you some of my work—I deal with metal mostly, cast and soldered bronze."

If Chalas were a real possibility for an upscale gallery like Goldstein's, an agent probably would have picked him up. But Mara believed talent existed in everyone and she had compassion for a person who struggled to make it in the competitive world of gallery art.

"We interview artists by appointment. For sculpture, slides and photos are required." She handed him a card with a smile. "Put a portfolio together and give me a call." There was no harm in giving the man a chance. "Now, about Lucas Naha—where does he live?"

The storekeeper gave her the directions.

Mara drove down a narrow branch that opened off the gravel road until she sighted a sprawling, comfortable-looking adobe house nestled behind a stand of cottonwoods. A dusty Jeep Comanche sat in the shade. Mara parked next to it, shut off her engine and stared at the house for a moment, thinking it looked nice but unexceptional.

Yet her pulse threaded unevenly. What on earth was the matter with her?

Taking a deep breath, she told herself to calm down, then she got out to knock on the door.

Eventually, an attractive older woman, gently rounded in both face and figure, appeared. "Yes, can I help you?"

"Hi, I'm Mara Fitzgerald...from the Goldstein Gallery in Santa Fe. I wondered if I could see Lucas Naha. Is he in?" She knew he should be. His agent had said that the artist rarely left the reservation.

The woman raised her brows. "Luke? Well, er...I have nothing to do with his business. I'm his mother,

Onida Naha." She swiped at one of the few strands of gray threading her black hair. "Luke is working out in the patio and doesn't want to be disturbed."

"Working on his paintings?" That sounded promising, as well as fascinating. "I would really like to talk to him for a moment."

"Well, I won't slam a door in someone's face, no matter how much Luke insists on keeping to himself."

Onida motioned for Mara to come inside, then headed down a hallway leading off on one side. Surprised, having thought she'd be told to wait while Naha was fetched, Mara followed the woman. Her eager gaze flicked over the furnishings they passed.

The successful artist didn't surround himself with luxury, though his home had large rooms and solidly built walls. A few small paintings hung here and there; a feathered kachina and a Catholic saint stood side by side in a niche. In the kitchen, Onida opened the back door that led out onto a tiled patio and a grassy area enclosed by an adobe wall.

The moment Mara spotted the painter working in the dappled shade of a cottonwood tree, she stopped dead in her tracks. Again, the weird sense of cognition made her anxious.

"Luke?" Onida called timidly.

The tall man continued to work intently, tubes of paint scattered around his feet. He either hadn't noticed the two women or wasn't paying any attention to them.

"Please don't disturb him," Mara told Onida before the woman could call to her son again. "I'll wait until he takes a break."

By then she would have drawn her thoughts together. They seemed to have scattered like the wind.

Onida nodded and went back inside.

Mara took a couple of steps forward, skirting an outdoor patio table. The painter was slashing a striking line of white into the azure background of the large canvas. Luke. The shortened version of his name was as strong as he appeared to be. His wide shoulders flexed beneath his dark T-shirt, and his hands looked powerful. His slim hips and hard thighs were encased in paint-spattered jeans, and his long black hair was tied back with a cord.

Oddly removed from the immediacy of the situation, Mara imagined herself untying the cord, running her fingers through the thick mane of hair. She could imagine it happening...almost as if it were a memory. The emotions pouring through her stunned Mara. She shuddered and wrapped her arms around her body to chase away a sudden chill.

Just as sudden, she met Naha's gaze when he whipped around, his dark eyes piercing, his lips set in a straight line. He came toward her. "Who the hell are you? What are you doing here?"

Unable to stop herself, Mara took a step backward. His tone was accusatory and his expression decidedly unfriendly. A thrill of fear pierced her even as she took in Luke's high cheekbones, straight nose curved at the tip, strong jaw, blue-black hair and lean, muscular body. She'd expected an aura of personal power, but she'd thought the artist would be older, not a virile man in his mid-thirties.

His eyes bored into hers and he raised his voice. "I said, *who* are you?"

"I'm Mara Fitzgerald." His intonation oddly reminded her of the same demand made in the weird dream. She felt as if she were dreaming now. "I've been looking forward to meeting you. I'm the new manager of Goldstein's—"

"The gallery?" He threw his paintbrush aside and stepped toward her, his manner threatening. "You're supposed to deal with my agent—that's what I'm paying him for."

Heart beating a bit too swiftly, she said, "I realize that."

He halted mere inches away, so she had to stare up into his hard, bronzed face. Instinct made her want to back up farther, but she forced herself to stand her ground. No matter that she told herself she wasn't afraid of him, the flesh along her arms responded with goose bumps. She sensed this man could be a truly fierce and dangerous enemy... or lover.

"What are you trying to prove?" he demanded, invading her space. "Do you think you can coerce me to finish the paintings faster?"

Mara had to force an answer. "Not exactly." Then she took a deep breath.

She doubted that anyone could pressure this man to do anything against his will. He possessed a truly fierce presence. A hard-bitten pioneer of the previous century would have turned tail and run if faced down by an Indian like Lucas Naha armed with so much as a butter knife.

"I'll be done when I'm done," Luke went on. "Gilbert Armijo should have told you that."

"He did." Though she wasn't about to let this man think she was intimidated. She straightened her shoulders and stared him in the eye. "I realize I'm overstepping my boundaries a bit here." How could she ask what she really wanted to—where did his inspiration come from, did his own imagery obsess him? "Umm, I want you to know how important your work is to the gallery. Your paintings present a unique vision of the Southwest—"

"Trying to pat me on the head?" Luke interrupted. "Real tactful, but it's not going to get you squat."

She bridled. "It's not empty praise. I'm being honest. And I'm not the only person who admires your work. You have a loyal following." She tried to ignore the way he was looming over her, the way she was having trouble breathing normally, the dribble of sweat wending a path down her spine. "Collectors are so inspired by your art that they believe the figures in your paintings are mystically alive and move around."

His expression suddenly went from threatening to surprised. "Figures moving around?"

"I was told they change position from time to time." Relaxing a bit now that she'd seemed to have some effect on him, Mara pointed out, "You have a mythos built around your artwork, an aura of mystery—"

But Luke's scowl was descending again. "Save the fancy words," he cut in, making her uptight all over again. "I don't give a damn what people believe about my paintings." He added, "And I want you out of here—right now."

So much for honesty and tact.

Before she could object, he grasped her arm and marched her none-too-gently toward a gate in the adobe fence. She couldn't believe he was actually manhandling her.

"Let go!" Pure anger burned away other, less heroic sensibilities. She tried to shake off his warm grasp. Which, even in this tense situation, gave her goose bumps that had nothing to do with fear. A sense of shared intimacy and a disappointment that she couldn't explain made her even angrier. "How dare you!"

He did release her when they reached the gate. "How dare *you!* I didn't invite you to my home." He gestured. "Your car's out there and the highway is right over the rise. I assume you can find your way back to Santa Fe."

She didn't bother to answer, merely started to stride away, her back stiff.

Luke wasn't finished. "Hey, aren't you going to warn me about a lawsuit, a breach of contract?"

Mara stopped short and turned. "Do you want me to threaten you?"

"I'd like to hear some real honesty."

Obviously he didn't believe anyone could possibly be pleasant or sincere. She stepped closer, daringly gazing into his eyes, trying not to get caught by the power there. "You deserve to be taken to court unless you meet the terms of your contract." She told herself that he couldn't affect her if she refused to allow it.

"Yeah?" He crossed his arms over his broad chest. "And are you worried about losing your job, maybe? Is that why you made the drive up here?"

Now she was too uncomfortable to mention her real reasons—not that he would believe them.

"I don't think you care about me or why I came here," she said tightly. "Not any more than you care about your many admirers, the people who collect your art. And you should. If you don't have enough output to keep collectors interested, they'll buy someone else."

"I paint for myself, not the money." Uncrossing his arms, he came closer, looming once more, making her aware of his disturbing maleness. "I don't give a damn about collectors."

Perhaps not. Swallowing hard, Mara glanced at the comfortable, if unassuming-looking house that was far nicer than anything else she'd seen around here. "If you don't care about the money for yourself, how about some for the other people of the pueblo? You could send several kids to college, help them find a positive path in life."

His bronzed skin darkened. "My family and people are none of your business."

Again, he reached out and took hold of her arm. His touch was less harsh, different this time. Surprised, Mara gazed up into his face, suddenly mesmerized by their closeness. The dark pupils of Luke Naha's eyes held mysteries she could lose herself in. Each one of his fingers seemed to burn into her flesh. As his warm expulsion of breath feathered her hair, her heart raced with an invisible connection that was raw and potent and as striking as a vivid memory....

She desired Luke Naha and he also wanted her.

She knew that to the depths of her core.

Both of them could have been frozen in place. Aeons seemed to pass before either of them could speak or act, could overcome the charged atmosphere that surrounded them. Finally an odd expression touched his features and he released her as abruptly as if he'd touched hot metal.

"Take your bleeding heart back to Santa Fe," he growled, stepping away.

Flustered, confused, a little stunned, Mara struggled to regain her wits. And control her body. Tingling sensations continued to spread along her limbs even though Luke was no longer touching her. Stomach churning with a combination of unwanted desire and justified hostility, she spun around to take hold of the gate handle.

"Wait! Luke, your grandmother would like your guest to stay."

Once more Mara halted, glancing over her shoulder to see Onida waving and hurrying across the patio.

"What?" The artist turned a questioning frown on his mother. "She's not my guest and she doesn't want to stay."

Obviously flustered, Onida slid her gaze from Mara to her son, then back again. "But I've made some tea—we can have refreshments out on the patio."

Mara was surprised by the new development. She started to make her own excuses in the uncomfortable situation when she noted the frail-looking, white-haired woman easing herself down into one of the patio chairs.

"She must stay, Luke," said the elderly woman, her strong, authoritative voice carrying.

Once more, Mara was filled with a strange sense of familiarity...and a compulsion to accept the invitation to tea that was every bit as strong as the urge to drive out here in the first place.

CHAPTER TWO

As she helped herself to homemade piñon, or pine nut, fritters, Mara focused on Luke's grandmother, wondering why the woman had wanted her to stay. Isabel Joshevama was blind, she realized, noting that the woman's eyes always seemed directed on some faraway inner scene. Dignified and handsome in spite of her years, she had obviously bequeathed her proud posture and elegant bone structure to her grandson.

"Luke, would you pass the piñon cakes?" Isabel asked.

"I'll put them on your plate, Grandmother. One or two?"

Mara nearly did a double take at such politeness. Considering he was of Pueblo heritage, however, born to a group that honored age, she knew she shouldn't be surprised that he treated his elders with respect. Luke pulled up a chair but remained silent, brooding and a bit disconcerting. Mara didn't know what to expect of him... or of herself.

No one had ever gotten to her as quickly or as deeply as Luke Naha had. It was more than his being a difficult artist. More than her being angry at his rude behavior. This was far more personal. More disturbing. She couldn't explain it. Her reaction to him was far too intense... and, at the same time, hauntingly familiar.

His mother smiled and poured tea while chatting about Spanish and Indian cooking. Onida seemed to possess a much sunnier, more open personality than her mother and son, but lacked their strong presence.

"Have you been here before?" Isabel suddenly asked Mara.

"To the reservation? No."

"I meant this part of the country."

Feeling as if Luke were staring right through her, Mara centered her gaze on his grandmother. Perhaps if she concentrated, she could ignore the effect he had on her. "This is the first time I've visited this area."

This answer didn't seem to satisfy Isabel. Her brooding expression made her resemble her grandson even more. Mara felt as if she were being sized up in a not-so-subtle way.

"What do you think of Luke's newest painting?" Isabel asked.

Luke's artwork. The reason she'd come.

Pulse thrumming, Mara glanced at the easel some yards away. "The one he's working on? Like his other paintings, it's stunning...mysterious, haunting... the type one dreams about."

Isabel frowned. "Dreams?"

Expression unreadable, Luke turned his full attention on Mara. "Now my paintings make people dream? I thought you said the mystery about them was that the figures moved around when nobody was looking."

"According to my assistant at the gallery."

Both Luke and Isabel seemed alert. The atmosphere was suddenly crackling with renewed tension.

Seemingly oblivious, Onida smiled and told her son, "I always think each painting is more beautiful than the last, Luke. I wouldn't know which to keep and which to give away if it was up to me. I'm glad you make those decisions." To Mara, she said, "I visit Goldstein's whenever he has a new collection. It's been awhile... but, of course, he's been busy with the murals at the community center."

"Murals?" Mara echoed.

"He's trying to make the reservation a nicer place—"

"Never mind about the murals," Luke cut in. "No excuses. If she wants to sue me for breach of contract, she can."

"Breach of contract?" Onida's hands fluttered nervously. "Oh, my."

"Actually, I'm not suing anybody—at least, not yet," muttered Mara, wanting to get back to the paintings and the dreams.

But Onida was clearly upset. "He's been so busy... and then there was the death of Victor Martinez. He was a clan elder."

"That's enough," Luke stated, though he touched his mother's arm gently to soften his order.

"Actually, it isn't." Frustrated, Mara told Onida, "I'm sorry for your loss," before turning back to Luke. "I want to get this out in the open—the mystery surrounding your paintings. That's what I've really been wanting to talk about. Does your imagery have something to do with Kisi mysticism? Does it obsess you, get into *your* dreams?"

Once again, Mara commanded both Isabel's and Luke's full attention. They seemed startled, especially Luke, and suddenly she wondered if he had recurring nightmares just as she did. Might that be why he was so isolated and angry? Is that why she felt this mysterious connection?

Luke rose. "I don't want to talk about dreams—or anything else." He glanced quickly at Isabel. "I think even Grandmother will agree it's time for you to leave."

The older woman said nothing, though Onida crumpled a paper napkin and laid it on the table. "You're being rude, Luke."

"It's rude to come to someone's home uninvited."

Deeply disappointed—she'd barely mentioned the topic in which she was so invested—Mara wasn't in the mood for more arguing. The tension really got to her. Gathering her purse, she scooted her chair back.

"It is late. I really should be going." The sun sank toward the western horizon. She told Onida, "Thanks for your hospitality."

"Will you return?" asked Isabel unexpectedly.

"I'm not sure." Though Mara wasn't certain that was an invitation, she made a point of saying, "I appreciate your asking."

She hated to lower herself to Luke Naha's level by being hostile but she couldn't help sniping at him when he followed her through the gate and out to her car.

"You don't have to strong-arm me again."

"I have no intention of touching you," he said, though his tense expression belied his words.

Nearly shivering at the thought of those long fingers touching her once more, Mara paused in the deepening shade of the big cottonwood tree. "You *do* have strange nightmares, don't you?"

He halted a few feet away and stared. She could hear him breathing. And knew she'd struck a nerve.

"I can tell," she went on, her pulse thrumming. "I suffer from nightmares, too. That's really why I came here. I dreamed about one of your paintings. It was so vivid, so strong.... Well, it frightened me."

"Forget about it."

"I can't forget."

His eyes were opaque, black as night. "You need to be careful, white lady. There are things in the universe that don't fit your neat little rules."

Then he turned abruptly and left her standing in the shadows, her breath coming in a gasp. Even more spooked—no doubt the reaction Luke had wanted—Mara glanced about before getting into the car. A light breeze whispered through the tree's leaves and the surrounding hills glowed with vivid colors. The light here seemed even clearer and more beautiful than in Santa Fe.

Yet the shadows beneath the tree were deep and dark. She carefully buckled herself into her seat, glancing all around before pulling out.

She wondered if Luke Naha was half as menacing as he would like her to believe. She hadn't exactly felt physically threatened, but the man had done an excellent job of playing on her inner fears.

Though alleviated by daylight and consciousness, the weird atmosphere of her dreams had followed her into Kisi country...an ambience which frightened and fascinated her at the same time.

Like Luke himself.

Which made her ponder the odd chemistry that bubbled between them. It was more than physical. Her emotions were high. How could she be so emotional about a stranger?

Mara drove toward the reservation's entrance, passing Tom Chalas's store, which was now closed. As usual in mountainous areas, twilight came quickly. Lights would be a good idea, yet she hesitated to switch them on until she pulled out onto the highway.

A few yards down, the beams picked up something white beside the edge of the road, and Mara stepped on the brakes, her heart sinking. An animal that had been run over? She hated roadkills. But she felt compelled to look, anyway. Gazing out the window, she saw that the body was that of a sheep...whose bloody throat gaped open.

A coyote rather than a car had obviously killed the poor thing. But how awful. In daylight? And so near the reservation?

She pressed down on the accelerator and sped away, pushing from her mind the horrible scene she'd just witnessed. Because his paintings were both profitable and beautiful, she hoped Luke's work would continue to be handled by her gallery. But personally, she'd had quite enough of Kisi mystery and mysticism, not to mention Lucas Naha himself, for the foreseeable future.

She only hoped his artwork would stay out of her dreams.

Early in the evening, a three-quarters moon rose over the Nacimiento Mountains as he reached his destination, a cabin built against the side of a rocky hill. A fire blazed, piercing the darkness, its yellow glow a portent of the evil he sought to harness.

Glancing back at the lights of the Kisi pueblo some miles away, he gunned his vehicle over the rutted road leading to the cabin, quickly parked it and headed for the fire.

"Olvera!" he called.

A Yaqui Indian with a scarred face rose from stoking the flames. "So...you've returned."

"I want to learn everything."

The man laughed. "Do you have enough money for everything? Power doesn't come cheap."

"I have money, witch, don't worry."

The Yaqui laughed again. "It will give me satisfaction to work with a Kisi—they brag about their ancient wisdom."

"I don't want to travel that road. It would take too long." Not that he didn't have some ability. "I want to destroy my enemies before they destroy me." As well as deal with invaders like the white woman who had been poking her nose around today. He pulled out a hundred-dollar bill. "Here's the first payment."

"Done." The Yaqui's eyes glittered as he snatched the money, stuck the bill in his pocket and took out some green cactus buttons to roll around in his palm. "You have the anger and the lust. All you need is the means to capture what you're seeking."

"Will that do it?" he asked, eyeing the peyote, a potent hallucinogen.

"Can a coyote kill a rabbit?"

He joined in when the Yaqui laughed this time. He had confidence in his choice of a teacher—Olvera was known far and wide as a dangerous witch, able to dominate the dark forces.

Although he had a healthy fear of the other man, he felt no guilt for using Olvera's knowledge to pervert the ways of the Kisi. Why not take the short path? He cared nothing about dreams of wisdom and ancient spirits. Anger had burned that away.

Olvera put the cactus buttons back in his pocket. "The time for this will come soon. Sorcery is stronger when the moon is full." He sat down in front of the fire. "Meanwhile, I can give you other suggestions."

He joined the other man, watching the flames, listening carefully as the witch told him what to do.

The sun had long fled when Luke awoke from a restless nap and went out the door of his personal living quarters to get some fresh air. Having painted since dawn, he'd been exhausted and had gone to his bedroom at dusk to lie down. Now it was late. He'd obviously slept through supper. Not that Onida wouldn't have something waiting on the stove for him, being used to his erratic work schedule. He strolled past the adobe-walled yard to the kitchen.

Dreams. He couldn't believe Mara Fitzgerald had brought up the topic during her visit today. He was certain her insistent, oddly perceptive nosiness was what had gotten under his skin, made him toss and turn...though, hopefully, he'd done nothing else during his nap.

On the other side of the yard, the Jeep Comanche sat in the same place. At least, as far as Luke could tell. He hadn't risen then to drive the vehicle somewhere while sleepwalking or in some other bizarre mental state—something that had happened a couple of times before.

Nightmares. Luke didn't even want to think about them.

He walked on, his boots crunching gravel. Some distance away, he saw a flashlight beam glimmering from the direction of the community center. Must have been some sort of meeting. Not that he'd been invited. When he'd agreed to do the murals for the center at his grandmother's insistence, the reservation's other citizens had been friendly for a while. But then a few individuals had persisted in trying to help out and his temper had gotten away with him. Now he worked alone.

He wasn't a people person, wasn't good at conforming with clan or tribal rules. He didn't particularly identify with the Kisi community, and they resented him for being a rampant individualist.

Though they'd more than resent him if they knew what had brought him back to the pueblo. They'd fear him if they learned why he'd left Arizona... that he might have been responsible for the fire that had consumed his home.

Brooding on that, he headed back toward the main part of his house, passing a neighbor's place. A startled face gazed out of a window, spotted him and quickly drew the curtains. They were turquoise, a color meant to ward off evil.

Maybe the community feared him now.

Sometimes he wondered why he *had* returned to the Kisi pueblo. He loved his widowed mother and cherished his wisewoman grandmother, but he had no more desire for a traditional way of life than the young people who fled the reservation.

Perhaps he'd returned simply because he'd needed a place to hide.

Luke went inside the house, passing his grandmother's bedroom and heading toward the kitchen. Since she hadn't been willing to abandon her home, he'd built the sprawling new one around these two rooms of her original adobe. A widow who'd been living in a trailer, his mother had been pleased to have a real house to fuss about again, and Luke had portioned off one wing of the place for his own use. He was happy that his artwork supported everyone, though he wasn't willing to lick boots to collect the money for his paintings—not even boots belonging to a beautiful woman.

He was still angry that Mara Fitzgerald had muscled her way into his abode today and disturbed everyone, especially him.

He was furious that he'd been so attracted to her.

Even now he could see the clarity of her eyes, as blue as a New Mexico sky; he could see her face, whose fine bone structure tempted an artist to capture it on canvas; he could see the shoulder-length golden brown hair that tempted a man's hands to slide through its thick silkiness.

Even now, he could feel the urgency that had made him want to kiss her, enter her, leave his mark in her.

Damn Mara Fitzgerald, especially the strange and confusing feelings she'd aroused in him. He nearly felt as if he knew her, as if they'd shared a past together....

Realizing his jeans tightened painfully, he adjusted his discomfort, forcing himself to put the disturbing woman out of mind at least for a while. He would think about her much later, when he was once again alone in his bed.

In the meantime, the kitchen's rich, spicy odors were making his mouth water. A pot of *posole*—hominy and pork stew—simmered on the stove and fry bread lay on a platter nearby. About to help himself, he heard voices coming from the living room.

Heading there, Luke saw that they had two visitors. Rebecca Harvier sat on the couch near his grandmother, her plump hands twisted in her lap, while his mother sat stiffly in the rocking chair across from the two elder ladies.

Charlie Mahooty stood near the center of the room, obviously having dropped by uninvited since nobody in the house liked him. "I'm gonna be the new governor of the Kisi. Everybody will vote for me, what with all this weird stuff going on."

"Weird stuff?" Luke scowled. If there was anyone he disliked in the pueblo, it was this bully. How dare the man issue a warning. "If by weird, you mean bad, I'd blame you."

Mahooty's thick lips formed a straight line. "I don't make witchlights float over the church at night, Naha. Or call up a big yellow coyote with glowing eyes. It killed a sheep today in broad daylight." He glared at Isabel and Rebecca. "Somebody is practicing witchcraft."

"Wise elders do not practice evil," answered Isabel. "They seek wisdom. They try to heal."

"Well, maybe you two are just too old to control yourselves anymore," said Mahooty. "Maybe you'd better hang up your prayer feathers."

Rebecca's eyes flashed behind her glasses. "Sacrilege! No one is ever too old to be a *finished person*." Her voice trembled. "You have no respect for the traditions of the Kisi and neither do the people who follow you. No wonder there are no more ceremonies in the kiva."

An underground chamber where the most sacred kachinas or statues of hallowed spirits were kept, the kiva had been the sacred space of the Kisi, as with all Pueblo-related clans.

Isabel added, "Furthermore, no one can become governor without the elders' approval."

Mahooty wasn't moved. "Maybe the laws are going to change. The tribal police named me captain, and I'm going to hold a vote at noon tomorrow. The people will take a look at the old laws and who should be governor. They will speak."

Isabel rose to face the man. Her voice was sharp. "Because they fear you, Charlie Mahooty. But your power is perverted—"

Flushed, Mahooty cut her off with a wave. "You don't tell me what to do, old woman. And you don't know anything about my power. Why, you're a dried-up old crow—"

Which was all Mahooty got out of his mouth before Luke took hold of him by the front of his shirt. "Don't speak disrespectfully to my grandmother or to Rebecca," he commanded, looming over the shorter man. "Or you'll answer to me."

"Settle down, Naha." Mahooty shook Luke off, though fear glistened in his eyes. "Why do you care about what the Kisi decide to do? You're rich—you can move to Santa Fe."

"But I don't want to. We're staying here." He pointed at the door. "And you're leaving this house right now."

Luke followed as the heavyset man walked down the hallway, the second person he'd escorted off his property today.

Mahooty stepped outside. "Better watch your grandmother, Naha, see that she doesn't wander too far. She could fall off a mesa one of these nights." He laughed.

Luke saw red and lunged for the other man. At the same time, Mahooty took off and Onida came running to the door.

"Please, Luke, no fighting."

Heart racing, muscles poised, he paused. "He threatened Grandmother. I should break his legs." *And maybe his head, too.*

"He's a stupid fool, Luke. He isn't worth it. Please, I don't want to lose anyone else in a brawl."

She was referring to the way Luke's father had died in a bar in Phoenix. Luke responded to his mother's pleading tone. Slowly releasing his breath, he turned and came back inside. He had to learn to control his temper.

Who knew what he was capable of when angry or disturbed? Even he didn't.

A short while later, Rebecca left, Luke walking her up the dark road to her house. On the way back, he took a good look around, sighting neither coyotes nor witchlights—floating, glowing balls created by sorcery.

Not that he would have to see them to believe that there was something decidedly wrong about the community lately. He might not be cheek-by-jowl with the inhabitants of the pueblo, but the dreamseeking training of his childhood, the powers of his grandmother, had shown him there were many levels of reality.

Levels Luke did not try to understand anymore and which he hoped had nothing to do with him at all.

Returning to the house, he went directly to his private quarters, settling down in his studio to gaze at his latest painting, seeking direction. A scuffling in the hallway warned of someone's approach. He drew a breath of relief when Isabel appeared in the doorway.

"You look tired, Grandmother," he said as she joined him on the couch. "You've been spending too much time in your dreaming place when you should be resting."

"Someone must do so, Stormdancer." Only Isabel ever called him the sacred name he'd taken at his manhood ceremony. "Mahooty was right about the old ways disappearing. Rebecca and I are the only corn priestesses left, the only *finished people*. There are no storm-bringer priests now that Victor Martinez is dead."

Luke muttered, "Perhaps the old ways *should* disappear."

Not that he wanted someone like Mahooty to cause that.

Isabel's blind eyes glittered. "Would you have evil destroy good, Stormdancer? There must be balance. The spirits entrusted us with sacred responsibilities." She took a deep breath. "Someone has invaded my dreaming place."

The sacred abode Isabel envisioned when seeking wisdom, the place that was based on a real spot that she'd always loved—Red Mesa. Only the Kisi knew how to dreamwalk. Only a *finished* Kisi should have the power to enter other's dreams or visions.

"Who, Grandmother?"

Isabel's voice wavered. "When I demanded a name, the invader would not answer." Her expression darkened. "I do not believe that Victor Martinez died a natural death."

A chill shot down Luke's spine and he stiffened. "You don't think he really had a heart attack in his sleep?"

"I believe he was stalked by someone with power. I fear that someone could be Charlie Mahooty."

Now he was really spooked. If someone with the morals of Mahooty turned his skills to evil, no one was safe. Luke remembered the warning about his grandmother going off a mesa.

"Why didn't you tell me this before?" he demanded.

"I wanted to find the right words to ask you what I must."

His heart sank. He knew what she was going to ask of him.

"I want you to dreamseek again, Stormdancer. You have always had the ability. You could be a stormbringer priest yourself."

"I don't even have a dreaming place."

Not to mention that he had a big problem with faith. He hadn't sought a true dream since he'd seen something dark and frightening within himself as a teenager. When his family had moved away from the pueblo and tradition, he'd been relieved.

But all his life, strange dreams had followed. Dreams that he hadn't always been able to remember. Dreams, as well as incidents, involving violence and destruction. . . .

"Stormdancer, the woman who was here today—"

"Mara Fitzgerald?" Luke tightened his jaw even as the name immediately conjured her image. "She wasn't invited. She was just trying to hurry up my painting."

"It was more than that. There was something else, something hidden, and it bothers me." Isabel absently rubbed the blanket-covered arm of the couch. "I sensed it—that's why I asked her to stay, even though you seemed to dislike her. She spoke so strongly of dreams. Why? Had she heard of Kisi legends?"

"I have no idea. I know nothing about her. Today was the first time I ever set eyes on her." Though something inside him put a lie to that statement.

"Is she part Indian, do you think?"

Another chord struck, but he said, "Her skin is as white as a sidewinder's belly."

"Your mother said she was very pretty."

Yeah, she'd been pretty. And he'd been attracted even if he didn't like her.

"Were her eyes brown?" Isabel queried.

"Blue. And I'm certain she doesn't have one drop of Indian blood." Wasn't he?

Isabel sighed. "Well, another mystery. But we can't afford the more serious kind. You are welcome in my dreaming place, Stormdancer. You are of my own blood. We can't waste time."

Again the chills. Mahooty's warning haunted him. He slung an arm about Isabel's shoulders, feeling the bones through her flesh, as fragile and light as a bird's. Her spirit was strong, but she wouldn't live forever. Though no one had better try to take her before her time.

"No one will harm you, Grandmother...not unless they want to answer to me."

"Then go to Red Mesa and dreamseek, Stormdancer." When he didn't reply, she became agitated. "Will you do as I ask?"

He sighed. "Yes."

Though Luke had no idea what could happen. Embracing his grandmother, he watched her leave, then gazed out the nearest window into the black night. He might as well be looking into his own soul. A dark, mysterious hole that he'd avoided for years. He wasn't sure he wanted to know exactly what was inside him, what terrible thing might have led him to destroy his wife and little son. He'd never been able to control his inner power.

If evil was stalking the Kisi pueblo, he only prayed it wasn't the blackness that lived within himself.

A ray of insistent light popped Mara's eyes open. She stared about, finding herself prone on the floor of a canyon. Again. For she had lain here before, wrapped in the same sheet.

At least this time she was wearing a nightgown.

She scrambled to her feet, dislodging a small stone. Her heart pounded, though she tried to control the foreboding feeling that clung to her like a shroud.

The sun hung low in the sky. The surrounding mountains were blue-violet, the chamisa and other brush darkening to shades of graying green. The crimson of the canyon's earth deepened to brick red. She glanced about nervously.

Night was fast coming on. She didn't want to stay in this eerie canyon when darkness completely descended. The overhanging cliffs lurked like predators, and the breeze hissed frightening whispers.

"Hello!" she shouted. "Is anyone here?"

Where was the Indian woman?

The question tore through her mind of its own volition. She moved forward, her surroundings shifting unnaturally. Gliding over rock and sand, she passed copses of piñon pine and juniper, speeding up until her breath came in spurts.

A red mesa suddenly loomed before her and she was just as suddenly atop it, looking down at her surroundings. The sun continued to sink, sending deep blue shadows creeping across the canyon. A star winked in the indigo sky high above, but its distant light was far too weak.

"Hello!" she shouted desperately.

And then subtle footsteps behind her froze her to the spot. She whipped about, her heart racing like a speeding deer.

A bare-chested Indian, hair loose to his shoulders, emerged from the semidarkness. Though he was tall and handsome, his shadowed expression frightened her, and his dark eyes burned right through her.

"You," he growled, *the single word both recognition and accusation. "Come to me."*

She shrank back.

"Stop," he ordered. *"I've been waiting too long."*

Too long.

Longing.

For longing—deep, wordless yearning—battled fear. Her eyes filled with tears. Her lips parted but she could not speak.

The stranger—yet somehow not a stranger—moved toward her, his glide silent, his muscles rippling. His mouth quivering with repressed emotion.

"You," he said again, *before pulling her to him.*

Pressing her tightly against his body, he raked his hands over her as if he owned her, as if he were memorizing every inch of flesh. She didn't resist. Couldn't. The familiarity about him kept her from fighting. He grasped the back of her neck so that her face turned upward.

His grip was so powerful, she knew he could snap her neck and kill her on the spot.

Instead, he savaged her mouth.

He. Not a nameless Indian, she realized, suddenly recognizing that she embraced Lucas Naha himself.

But Luke was also something—someone—else....

Her thoughts muddled as her own passion took over her consciousness, blooming into full, ripe flower. Moaning, she let her head drop back, wrapped her arms about her lover's neck and rocked her hips against him. Her satin-covered nipples were tight little buds carrying heat and sensations to and from her lower belly.

Her lover growled deep in his throat, throwing the sheet aside and pulling her lacy, cream-colored night-gown up to slide his hands along her naked flesh. She could feel the proof of his desire pressing hard against the material he wore about his waist, the only barrier between them.

She wanted him, desired him with all her heart and soul. She pulled back slightly so he could cup her breasts, hold the soft weight of them and flick his thumbs over her sensitive nipples.

She shuddered, panting, her knees nearly giving way.

Understanding her need, he lowered her to the ground, continuing to kiss her deeply, to caress her. Their tongues touched, their breaths blended. He parted her legs, arranged himself between them, stroked and teased her until she writhed, begging him to take her.

He understood, though she was speaking strange-sounding words she didn't understand. A dark profile against the dream blue sky, he answered her in the same strange tongue, started to remove the barrier so they could become one. . . .

A strange language.

A familiar man.

But familiar how?

She drew back slightly, raised herself to her elbows to gaze hard at her lover. At Luke Naha. Once again, she had the strong sensation that he was someone else...and that she was also someone else...someone who couldn't remember her real name.

Impatient, he pushed her back to the ground with more guttural words.

Fear suddenly laced her passion. He was so strong, so overwhelming that she stiffened. "Wait."

He ignored her until she shoved her hands between them and put pressure on his chest. "I said wait. This is going too fast."

Though he allowed her to halt him, fury blazed across his craggy, bronzed features. Then he rose, and some of the tension drained from her...until he stepped back, one foot following the other, receding quickly while his image started to fade.

"Wait," she cried again, this time desperate for a renewal of his touch. As if angered by her very reluctance, he disappeared, blending into the shadows creeping across the mesa. "Don't leave me!"

But he had already gone.

After staring about wildly for a moment, she curled back against the earth to weep because she was confused, afraid.

And because she was so alone.

Mara awakened sobbing, heart pounding, tears streaming down her cheeks. Her nightgown bunched up about her shoulders, she was also wet with sweat and shamelessly aroused.

Was she going mad?

Struggling out of bed, she pulled down her slippery nightgown and rose on shaky legs. This dream had been even more soul-shattering than the last, with fleeting, warring thoughts and emotions—desire, fear, passion, grief.

Grief?

Mara wasn't sure where that feeling had come from.

Though she was positive it had been Luke Naha she'd nearly made love with.

Luke Naha.

First it had been his painting, and now he himself who had invaded her dreams. And she'd wanted him, ached for his body.

A dream lover.

For Mara knew she would have capitulated if the man in her passion-drenched night fantasy had continued with his seduction, if he hadn't become so angry when she'd told him to wait that he'd faded from her vision.

She mourned for a stranger... for the achingly familiar emotions he'd stirred in her.

What power did this man hold over her?

CHAPTER THREE

Luke came out of his trance at dawn, with the morning sun climbing the eastern mountains. Highly aroused, he took a deep breath of the clean, piñon-scented air and tried to ignore the physical discomfort pressing hard against his jeans.

Some wiseman he was. Sent to search for a high vision to help his grandmother, he'd come up with a teenager's wet dream.

The only plus was that he could now tell Isabel who had been invading her dreaming place. The elderly woman was sure to be stunned.

Luke himself felt astonishment mix with the other sensations and memories zinging through his consciousness....

Mara Fitzgerald writhing beneath him, her smooth skin sliding beneath his fingertips, her soft mouth opening to his ministrations...

Enough. He already needed an icy cold shower.

Stiff from sitting in one position so long, he got to his feet, strode across the mesa and quickly maneuvered the steep path leading down the opposite side. Then he hurried for his house, planning to enter directly into his quarters. He didn't want to talk to anyone until he had calmed down and gathered his thoughts.

* * *

As he'd expected, his grandmother registered open shock when he met with her later that morning in his studio.

"So it was the white woman in my dreaming place." Isabel's blue-veined hands gripped the arms of the couch. "I—I had an unusual feeling about her, but I didn't think this was possible."

Luke touched her frail shoulder, trying to comfort her. "I saw her, Grandmother. She was even wearing the striped sheet you described." And a lot less after he'd ripped it off her.

Isabel said faintly, "A white woman. What does this mean? Only the Kisi are able to dreamwalk. Only the wise...or very clever evil spirits...witches," she said, voice trembling.

Mara Fitzgerald was no witch, Luke felt certain. "I sensed no evil in her," he said truthfully. Just fear and passion.

"Tell me the vision, every detail," Isabel ordered.

That would take some editing. Luke sat back in his own chair. "Well...she appeared on Red Mesa, she had this sheet wrapped around her..."

"And?"

"She was also wearing a nightgown." A satiny confection which he had nearly whipped over Mara's head. He'd seen the whole display, anyway—beautiful breasts, nicely rounded hips, long shapely legs. Desire stirring again, he steeled himself. "She saw me...and seemed surprised."

She'd appeared to be as stunned as he'd felt and also hauntingly familiar, like they'd met more than once before.

"Stormdancer." Isabel's stern tone shook him out of his musings. "Did the woman say anything?"

"Nothing I could understand."

"She didn't speak English?"

"No." Now that he thought about it, "It sounded more like Kisi."

Which he was no expert in. He had always felt lucky if he could understand the words uttered by Isabel or other elders during religious ceremonies.

"Kisi." Isabel leaned forward, her frown deepening. "Yet you do not believe the woman is a witch? You are withholding something, Luke. I can feel it."

He wasn't about to go into more vivid detail with his grandmother.

"Look, I don't know why this woman got into my dream," he insisted, knowing he sounded defensive. "And I don't know how." He wasn't even certain what had stopped them from mating. "She was just there, okay? There was nothing I could do about it."

Isabel sat so quietly, Luke wondered if he'd offended her. He watched her relax, slowly compose her features.

Finally, she announced, "You must go fetch this woman, Luke." He opened his mouth to object, but she went on. "I must speak to this Mara Fitzgerald. Bring her to the reservation."

Oh, yeah. "And what if she doesn't want to come?"

"Use whatever means you must to bring her to me."

Luke stared at a painting resting against the wall, a plan starting to form in his mind. "All right. I'll bring her—if nothing else, to make sure all this trouble gets dealt with."

Including his having to seek visions. Maybe talking to Mara Fitzgerald would help his grandmother decide how to overcome the dangers she'd been worried about.

But to get Mara here, Luke knew he would probably have to eat crow enchiladas, something he wasn't looking forward to.

Mara smiled at Tom Chalas, fighting off annoyance. Yesterday, she'd distinctly told him that he needed to make an appointment to present his artwork, but he'd just shown up unannounced and unexpected barely twenty-four hours later.

Mara knew she could better deal with the situation if she wasn't still feeling wrung out by her newest dream.

"I have quite a few slides and photos," Chalas was saying, "so I didn't want to delay getting them to you."

His fingers trembled slightly as he unzipped the portfolio. Though pushy, he was also vulnerable and obviously desperate. Mara's annoyance faded, replaced by sympathy. Unfortunately, it was difficult to be encouraging about the pieces in the photos that Chalas spread out on the desk.

"Hmm, interesting." Actually, rather hostile looking with bristling spearlike points and snarling metal masks. The abstract bronze pieces definitely didn't appeal to Mara, but even if their basic concept had, their design and execution were rather crude. What was she going to say? "Something about them reminds me of war—helmets, swords, spears."

"War. That's exactly the idea I was aiming for," said Chalas enthusiastically. "There's always been so much conflict in New Mexico, the clash of cultures." He pushed a photo in front of her. "This is my newest piece."

It was a little different, if not any more expertly done. The piece was off-putting, resembling a figure loaded down with chains.

"This reminds me of . . . well, enslavement." And it gave her the creeps. But she struggled to keep an open mind.

Chalas was trying hard. He acted pleased rather than put off. "Most of us are chained down in this world—that's what I was trying to put across. You have an incredible eye."

Mara attempted diplomacy. "Have you tried to get any other galleries to represent your work or sold any pieces on your own?"

Chalas tightened his jaw. "A few."

From his tone, she could tell he hadn't gotten a good response from either galleries or potential collectors. And no wonder. But her art therapy background made her believe that positive creativity dwelled in everyone.

"You might want to redefine your ideas," she said. "Try developing the war idea into a grander statement about the horror and agony that humanity has suffered through the years, about how terrible it is to kill one another."

Though she doubted the solution was so simple. Change had to come from within the artist himself before his work could have a more positive effect on the viewer. Chalas's sculptures seemed to be a reminder of some terrible conflict, but didn't speak against it.

The man grabbed the acetate sheet and scooped up the photos. "So you're saying you won't represent these pieces?"

"I don't think you're quite ready for a major gallery at this time, Mr. Chalas. But keep working—"

"Until when?" he interjected, anger edging his voice. "I've been working at this for twenty years." Anger glinted from his eyes. "Maybe I should go back to the pueblo and whip up some wind chimes, or, better, carve a few kachina ornaments for people to hang on their Christmas trees."

"I'm sorry."

Chalas charged out of the office, nearly colliding with Felice Paquin. "Excuse me," she squeaked, her blue eyes wide.

Which was unlike the usually unflappable Felice, Mara thought.

Tom Chalas didn't bother apologizing. Intending to have a talk with her assistant, Mara rose and poked her head out to make sure the man was leaving. That's when she caught sight of what had really flustered Felice.

Or rather, *who.*

Luke Naha lounged near the reception desk, a bundle of canvases beside him, his arms folded across his broad chest. His strong features passive, he stared curiously at Chalas, who glared back in passing, his expression filled with resentment...and perhaps hatred.

Then Luke turned his unsmiling black gaze on the women, focusing on Mara. Caught by surprise, she let her mouth drop open, then started backing away, memories of her erotic dream this morning returning with exquisite clarity and causing her to blush furiously.

She ran into her office.

What a circus. Joining the fray, Felice followed, her expression now worried.

"What's going on? Are you all right?" Felice went on excitedly, "Lucas Naha is here to deliver some paintings, and he says he wants to talk to you. Incredible. What did you do to him out on the reservation?"

The question was what *he'd* almost done to *her*. But that had only been a dream, her conscious mind lectured reasonably. And she'd have to forget about it if she was going to face him with any sense of dignity.

"I didn't do anything to Naha," Mara gasped, trying not to panic, "except talk to him for a while. Maybe he's come to his senses on his own."

"Wow." Felice stared at her with open admiration.

"Give me a minute." Mara straightened her shoulders, smoothed her long, flowing printed skirt, tried to slow her pounding heart. She gestured to the door. "Tell him to sit down and wait. I'll let you know when you can show him in."

Felice left, closing the door behind her, and Mara sank down into her chair.

Wait. Hadn't she demanded he wait in her dream? Mara mused. Was she again experiencing déjà vu? Reality and fantasy seemed to be madly crisscrossing paths.

She closed her eyes, took some slow deep yoga breaths she'd learned in a stress seminar at the hospital she used to work for. But they only calmed her a little. When she rose, her knees were sponge. And when she opened the office again, motioning to Felice, she still wasn't ready for Luke Naha.

Would she ever be?

She made sure that the desk lay between them as he entered and sat down. The room filled with his presence—strong, highly intoxicating. She wasn't sure if the latter was what made him so scary. Her face hot, she knew she was blushing again and hated herself for it.

She glanced at him quickly, then stared at the ink blotter on her desk top while fingering the edge. He was wearing a white shirt open at the throat, and blue jeans with a fancy silver-buckled belt. His hands—strong, long-fingered, callused but artistic—lay quietly on the arms of the chair.

She recalled exactly what those hands had felt like as they'd touched and stroked and explored her....

She cleared her throat. "You've brought in some paintings, I hear."

"Only four. Take a look at them if you want."

"I'm sure they're wonderful," she told him, still playing with the blotter. "I'm so happy you decided to let us have them. And I assume there are even more in the process of being completed."

"I guess you can assume that all right."

She forced herself to glance at him, noting his narrowed eyes. "So what did you want to talk about?"

"You need to come out to the pueblo," he said quietly but firmly.

Now, caught by his intense gaze and urgent tone, she did stare at him. "Excuse me?"

He leaned forward. "I said you need to come out to the pueblo."

She couldn't believe it. "Why? So you can serve me some more tea, then kick me off your property a second time? You're crazy."

"It's important."

"That's what Isabel said yesterday." And she was having no more of this.

His jaw hardened and he made a low frustrated sound.

But he leaned even closer. "Look at me, Mara. Really look at me."

His voice was mesmerizing. His eyes were dark, hauntingly fathomless pools. She could almost lose herself in them. She *had* lost herself in them before—she was sure of it—but when?

He repeated his demand. "You *will* come to the pueblo."

She seemed to see him through a haze, hear him though an echo chamber. "The pueblo."

"We'll leave right now. Grandmother needs to see you."

She automatically reached for the drawer in which she'd placed her purse. "I will come to the pueblo and we're leaving right now?"

He nodded and rose, looming over her.

The physical threat made her move back in her chair.

And broke the spell.

Coming out of the haze, she frowned up at him. "What's going on here? Are you trying to hypnotize me? I'm not going anywhere—"

Which was all she got out before he took hold of her chin, raising her face to him. "*Look* at me."

She felt the pull—part of her wanted to obey—but her anger allowed her to brush him away. "Stop it. Keep your hands off me!"

He scowled, but straightened, giving her a little space. "That's not what you wanted last night, Miss Prissy Pants. You not only wanted my hands on you, you were begging me to take you."

For the second time that day, Mara's jaw dropped. She rolled her chair backward until it smacked into the wall, startling her. "Wh-what are you talking about?"

"You know what I'm talking about. Our mutual dream."

Her heart pounded wildly. Oh, God. He knew. He must.

She felt as if she'd been stripped naked. Again. And realized the enormity of his implication. "W-we couldn't have had the same dream. That's impossible."

"In white men's philosophy, maybe. Not in the Kisi's." Eyes sliding over her with familiarity, he asked, "Where did you get that little tattoo on your shoulder, anyway? A blue snake? You don't seem to be the type."

He'd seen her naked all right. "I—I got it when I was in college." On a whim. But tattoos were hardly the issue. She stood. "How dare you. You can't just march in here and make demands. And you can't—"

"Enter your dreams?" His smile was cool. "Think again, white lady. You walked into *my* dream, my territory. What were you doing on Red Mesa?"

She had no answer for that, no explanation as to how anyone could enter anyone else's dreams. The entire concept was foreign, mind-boggling. As well as utterly fascinating. It hit a nerve deep, deep down.

But all she could say was, "I don't understand."

"That's why you need to talk to Grandmother. She'll tell you all about dreamwalking." He reached for her, dragging her out and around the desk. "Let's get going."

Again, fear feathered her insides, but whether she was afraid of him or of what she might learn, she couldn't say. "Take your hands off me."

A familiar expression of anger crossed his features. "I'm getting tired of hearing that. You like my hands," he said, pulling her to him, pressing her against the lean length of his body. "Admit it."

And God help her, she did. Mara tried to ignore the sensations coursing through her, tried to pretend she didn't want him with every fiber of her being.

Only the door bursting open snapped her out of what would surely have ended in more than an illusory kiss.

Felice stood there, staring. "Mara?"

What must her assistant think, seeing her embracing Luke Naha? Mara managed to push away from him. Her own mind raced fast and furious.

She was surprised at the direction it was taking. "I'll be going out to the Kisi pueblo this afternoon to check on some more of Luke's paintings, Felice," she said, trying not to think of the decision as giving in to his will. "And I'll need you to take care of the gallery while I'm gone."

"Of course."

"Something has come up."

Staring at Luke, Felice raised her brows. "So I see. Don't worry, I'll take care of everything and lock up tight at six."

Mara turned to Luke. "Shall we be going?"

For even though she feared and disliked him, Mara rationalized to herself that she desperately wanted to find out everything possible about this dreamwalking business.

She wanted it with almost as much passion as she desired the man himself.

Mara Fitzgerald made no objection to taking his Jeep, Luke was glad to note. But she started having a hissy fit as soon as they climbed into the vehicle.

"If you ever grab me like that again, threaten me or push me around, so help me, I'll . . . I'll shoot you!"

He glanced toward her curiously as he turned the ignition key, noting the glittering eyes, the flushed skin that made her look even more beautiful than when calm. "You got a gun?"

"Not yet, but I'll buy one and put a bullet right through your skull!"

Though he could tell she was just about angry enough to do it, he had to smother a grin. The woman had courage, as well as strength. He had attempted to use a Kisi voice command on her in the office and she'd resisted. But then, maybe he hadn't quite gotten the hypnotic technique right, since he'd learned it from a storm-bringer priest as a kid and had rarely tried to use it through the years. Still, she was someone to be reckoned with, even if she didn't seem to have any idea of how she was able to dreamwalk.

Mara stared daggers at him as he circled Santa Fe's central plaza. "No more threats, no manhandling—I want your agreement before I go out to the pueblo."

He nearly told her it was too late now that she was in his truck. But she was so furious and so adamant that he decided to be amenable.

"Okay, I'll keep my hands to myself." Which wouldn't be easy. There was enough electricity between them to light up the whole state. He added sarcastically, "And maybe I'll try to watch my mouth."

She took a deep, huffy breath and settled down some. After a few blocks, she said, "I guess I can live with that. If you mean it, that is. I wasn't joking about shooting you."

"I know."

She glanced out the window and gestured. "I live right around the next corner. I'll need to stop by my apartment before we head out. I want to change into something more comfortable and take along a wrap. It's colder up north."

True, especially after dark. Though Luke hoped Mara wouldn't be staying into the evening. She might be enticingly attractive, unusual and fascinating, but unless she wanted to warm his bed for a few hours, he intended to see her off the pueblo as soon as possible.

He turned down the street she indicated, slowing as he approached a new condo complex of red adobe that was fronted by shallow, Spanish-style, wrought-iron balconies.

"Here?"

"Right." She had her hand on the door handle as he braked to a stop. "I'll be back in a minute."

"I'm not waiting out here. I'll go with you."

Her blue-gray eyes looked startled, then fearful. "I don't want you in my place."

For some reason that hurt. And her fear again made Luke angry. He wasn't a rapist or a murderer.... Well, at least he'd never tried to kill anyone intentionally.

He carefully controlled his temper. "You were treated with hospitality in my house. You can't do the same for me?"

"Hospitality, ha. It was your mother and your grandmother who offered me tea, not you. And you still ended up telling me to hit the road."

"I'm not going to hurt you." He *wanted* to go inside, wanted to see her place, examine her belongings. "I won't touch you. You've already got my word on that."

She sighed. "All right, then, I guess."

They entered the building silently and took the stairs up to the second floor. He kept several feet of non-threatening space between them as they headed down a hallway. Mara stopped at a doorway and unlocked it, glancing at Luke only a little apprehensively as he followed her in.

"I'm going to get dressed," she reiterated, gesturing toward the couch in the living room. "You can make yourself comfortable out here."

But as soon as she disappeared down a short hall, closing a door behind her, Luke started moving about, curious to see if Mara Fitzgerald's belongings would shed any light on her unusual ability to dreamwalk.

Her living quarters were neat and well lit, with big sliding glass doors to the balcony dominating one wall of a combination living and dining room. A kiva-style fireplace was built into another wall and an efficiency kitchen bordered the dining area. The hallway probably led to a bath and a couple of bedrooms. The modern furniture was pale and tasteful and new looking.

Uninterested in low-slung couches or bleached-wood dining room sets, Luke examined Mara's more personal belongings, fingering a Pueblo pot sitting on the shelf of a bookcase and then skimming the titles of her books.

Mixed between hardback and paperback novels were texts on art therapy, a creative way to work with mental patients using art. Luke had heard about that. On the lowest shelf, he found more than a dozen books on understanding dreams, including worn-looking tomes by Carl Jung and more modern manuals that touched on creative visualization.

So Mara *had* been interested in dreaming for some time. Stepping away from the bookcase, Luke flipped through the magazines lying on the glass coffee table and found a slim oversize paperback on Southwestern Indian myths.

Still, Mara couldn't have learned to dreamwalk from any combination of the materials she possessed. Luke headed for the walk-in efficiency kitchen, running his hand along the counters and stopping to gaze at a small framed drawing above the kitchen table. A portrait of a woman done with pastels, the face had an otherworldly look, and the background seemed to explode with color. The *M.F.* in the corner of the drawing told Luke that Mara herself had executed the drawing. He wasn't surprised—people in art-related occupations usually participated in the process themselves.

Thirsty, he took a glass from the cupboard, then decided to check out the refrigerator. Empty, except for a couple of cans of soda and some fruits and vegetables. Opting for soda over water, Luke was taking a swig and inspecting the collection of coffee mugs hanging above the sink when Mara reappeared.

"What are you doing?" she asked from the doorway of the kitchen, her tone distinctly unfriendly.

Luke glanced at her, noting the form-fitting jeans she now wore with a bright blue blouse. The color flattered her complexion and her golden brown hair, making her eyes seem more intense. "I was thirsty."

"So you just helped yourself?"

"Politeness isn't one of my virtues."

"Meaning you have some?"

He liked it when she really got her back up. "I'm a good artist. You've admitted that yourself. That could be counted as a virtue, I guess."

"I guess." She set the sweater she carried over the back of a kitchen chair. "I've got to... comb my hair before we leave."

Which probably meant she was planning on visiting the bathroom.

"Fine," he said agreeably and acted like he was starting back for the living room.

She skittered off before he could pass by her too closely and he heard the bathroom door slam. Now he'd have a chance to look in her bedroom, he thought, silently gliding down the dark hallway. The infamous striped bed sheets were the first items that caught his eye.

Interesting—sometimes a dreamwalker envisioned objects from his everyday world and took them along.

Inhaling the faint drift of perfume and body lotions, recalling his erotic vision again, Luke stared at the bed, finally noticing the shimmer of cream-colored satin near one of the pillows. Mara's nightgown, the one he'd nearly gotten off her. He moved closer to pick up the slippery garment, once again appreciating the lace trim at the bodice.

But it had been the curvaceous body beneath the nightgown that had really aroused him. The body of a stranger...and yet so familiar... Growing hard while fingering the satin, Luke couldn't help bringing it close to his face so he could inhale Mara's enticing odor.

"Put that down!"

She'd sneaked up on him again. Luke had been distracted, especially in the bedroom, or his keen sense of hearing would have picked up her footsteps.

Mara's face had turned a brilliant red. "I said put it down."

Luke casually dropped the nightgown on the bed. "Okay, but you aren't going to wipe out what happened this morning, no matter how bad you want to." Not knowing exactly why he was angry, he stepped toward her aggressively. "And a dreamwalker would never do anything in a vision that he wouldn't do in real life. You like me—you kissed me like crazy. You rubbed yourself against me like a cat in heat."

She backed up. "Stop it."

He stood still, realizing he was acting threatening again. "Got something against Indians?"

She took a deep, shuddering breath, seemed to draw herself together. "Your race has nothing to do with it, Luke. I've seen many attractive Native Americans. I simply dislike you personally."

"It's not like I want to get involved."

"Oh, you're only interested in a roll in the hay? Well, forget it. You're macho and crude, not to mention that you seem to possess one of the nastiest temperaments in the Western hemisphere." She glared. "Now get out of my bedroom."

Right. They should be going, anyway. She walked down the hallway, her back very straight.

Luke followed, unable to keep from needling her. "You must think macho and crude is hot stuff at some level—"

She whipped around. "Will you please quit bringing up the stupid dream? I felt desire, all right? Lust— whatever you want to call it. I don't know where it came from, but I can't be completely responsible for my unconscious feelings." She added, "And I'm certainly not going to act on them. I'm far more interested in how we could possibly have had the same dream in the first place."

Gazing at her, Luke suddenly became aware of the painting hanging on the wall beside her. He could hardly believe his eyes. Forgetting about what they were discussing entirely, surprise nearly replacing the sexual tension hanging in the air, he growled, *"Lightning Over Red Mesa.* Where did you get this?"

"I bought it—at the San Francisco Goldstein Gallery. I worked there part-time all the way through college."

Luke reached out to flip on the wall switch nearby. Track lighting glowed overhead. Once again, the painting came alive, just as it had when he'd worked on it. "I did this years and years ago, back when I still lived in Arizona." And right after his wife and son had died. "I saw it in a dream and it called me home. I knew New Mexico was the only place left for me."

Which gave him goose bumps. What was the painting doing in Mara Fitzgerald's possession?

"Called you home?" she murmured, also staring at the painting. "You dreamed about this painting, too?"

"That's where I get a lot of my ideas for my paintings." When he wasn't having nightmares. "I use any visionary power I have for my art."

"Visions? Is dreamwalking done while you're sleeping or is it a type of meditation?"

"It's done both ways. Though the wise use it intentionally, so I guess you'd say that was closer to meditation."

"The wise?"

Though he'd told her his grandmother would explain everything, he somehow didn't mind her asking. She couldn't help but be curious. "Dreamwalking is a skill that's passed down from one generation to the next by the Kisi."

"Then how did I—?"

"That's what we need to find out. We've never known of anyone who could just choose to dreamwalk at will. People have to learn how to do it—it's used by the wise to heal or seek wisdom, offer protection." He mused, "Of course, any power can also be reversed, as well, controlled by those who seek to do evil."

For a moment, Mara was silent. They both stared at *Lightning Over Red Mesa,* Luke noting that the tiny figure he'd painted in the first place did indeed seem to be in a different position. The hairs on the back of his neck stood on end. Was the mythos surrounding his art actually real?

"I don't want to do evil," Mara told him. "I don't think that's why I got into your dream."

"I know you're not evil."

"You do?"

"I would be able to sense it if you were." About himself, however, he wasn't sure at all. "But let's get out of here. My grandmother will be better at explaining."

Having gotten closer while looking at the painting, he heard her swallow. "Should I be afraid?"

When dreams often scared the hell out of Luke himself? But he said, "I don't think so. There's got to be some kind of explanation."

"I feel so mixed-up." She gestured to the painting. "I've been there twice, you know. I saw an Indian woman the first time, then you." She paused, swallowing again. "There were so many emotions. I woke up crying my heart out, like I'd lost someone, something—"

He could feel her pain, like a strange, deep grief was stirring within him, as well. As if he, too, felt more than the instantaneous attraction. As if they'd known each other before.

He didn't want to take the time to understand. Instead he touched Mara's shoulder, then realized he'd given his word to keep his hands off her.

"I forgot," he said, withdrawing.

But she hadn't gotten uptight. In fact, her mood had changed completely. She had a dreamy look as she turned, drifting forward to slide her hands up his chest. Surprised, he just stood there. Her hands stopped when they reached his face. Her lips trembled and tears stood in her eyes.

Again, the strange grief stirred within him. Mixed with longing. He felt compelled to react, to take her in his arms. She moaned as he suddenly pulled her against him and raised her mouth for his kiss.

CHAPTER FOUR

Luke molded Mara against him, kissing her deeply, running his fingers through the silk of her hair. She felt so good, like she belonged in his arms. They fit together perfectly. His heart thudded against his ribs when she wrapped her arms tightly about his neck and opened her mouth to him. Their tongues touched, the contact fiercely exciting. Pressed against his chest, her nipples pebbled, telling him without words that Mara experienced the same thrill.

Only minutes before, he'd had his guard up with this woman. Now he was lost to everything but the sensations of holding her, plying her with insistent kisses. She was so receptive, so enticing. He wanted to scoop her up in his arms and carry her right back to the bedroom. Seriously tempted to do just that, he tightened his hold.

She made another soft sound and squirmed a little, stopping him from going further. Then she placed her hands against his chest and pushed herself away, looking dazed... and a bit horrified.

The sudden loss of contact was like a rush of ice water.

"No," she said, her face suddenly closing.

Luke fought frustration and let go of her. "Damn it, woman."

She stepped back, her breasts rising and falling softly as she let her breath slow. "I don't know how we got into this."

He was having trouble catching his breath himself. And controlling his too-easy anger. "Of course, you blame me, the manhandler."

"No." Face flushed, she backed up farther. "I realize it was my fault—I don't know what got into me."

At least she wasn't making it out to be all his doing.

Anger dissipating, he scowled anyway. "What's the matter with you? Are you schizoid or something?"

"If you're trying to say I have a split personality," she said tightly, "the correct terminology is disassociative personality disorder."

He hadn't thought she might be crazy before, but now he was beginning to wonder.

"I would be a very unique case," she went on, her beautiful brow furrowed, obviously taking the criticism seriously. "Since I only change identities in my dreams."

"Yeah, and are you dreaming now?"

"I... No." Then she made a dismissive gesture. "But talking about dreams got me into this situation in the first place."

She glanced at *Lightning Over Red Mesa*, then turned away to pick up her fuzzy blue-and-brown sweater. Her purse had been hanging on the doorknob and she slid it over her shoulder.

"Can we go? I guess I need to talk to Isabel."

They headed out, Mara locking her apartment behind her. Luke wasn't sure what to believe. This woman was a puzzle, an enigma. He didn't understand her motivations, not to mention her special abilities.

All Luke knew was that she could push his buttons with the swing of her hips, the smallest quiver of her pretty mouth. She had too much power over him. He wished he could either out-and-out have her or find some way to keep his distance when he wanted to. That he could do neither left him frustrated and angry. He hated feeling like a randy teenager around her.

Maintaining an uneasy silence, they climbed into the truck and took the main highway north out of Santa Fe. One of the oldest cities in the U.S., it was a charismatic mix of low-slung, aged adobe buildings and newly constructed replicas, some of which were vacation homes for movie stars and other wealthy people from L.A.

Mara stared at a fancy new development on the outskirts of town, thinking the attached town houses rambling up a rocky hill resembled cliff dwellings. But the housing development was only a pleasant distraction. Reality returned as they left the city limits.

Ancient mountains and wild foothills loomed in the distance. Anxiety warred with an odd sort of excitement inside Mara.

She glanced at Luke, his profile stern against the bright daylight beyond the truck. Her heart beat faster with the combination of excitement and fear. Had she been foolish to simply pick up and leave with him?

Despite their mutual antagonism, she couldn't help feeling her actions were justified. And being with him satisfied her on more than a physical plane.

But why? Because this dreamwalking business might finally resolve her problems with nightmares? Could mysticism explain something that science couldn't? For she'd left psychology behind in the dry New Mexico dust when she'd learned that Luke had also dreamed of Red Mesa....

"So you don't think you're crazy, huh?"

His voice shook her out of her musings, reminding her of the man's all-too-real physical presence. She wished she could treat their strange, heady attraction with as much casualness as he could. He'd seemed more irritated than unnerved when she'd pulled away from their kiss. On the other hand, she'd been nearly devastated, and had pushed away from him to protect herself.

A difficult thing to do when he turned and affixed her with a dark, disconcerting gaze, which made her struggle to remember his question.

"I don't know if I'm crazy or not," she said breathlessly. Even a look left her confused and bubbling with some unnamed emotion. "But I've never read about sharing a dream with someone else in any psychology textbook."

"How about parapsychology?"

"I never took a course on that," she admitted. "It wasn't a requirement. Plus it kind of...scares me."

"Why?"

The fear was elemental, something she didn't want to explore too closely. "There aren't any real explanations for special mental abilities like telepathy and so forth."

"So you want everything easy to figure out."

"Psychology isn't necessarily easy," she said, irritated by his nonchalant accusation. He always seemed to be on the attack. "But at least it makes an attempt at explaining things for us." She decided to do some explaining herself. "I used to have terrible nightmares from time to time as a child. I'd wake up screaming and sobbing. My parents tried to help, but all they could do was comfort me."

"What were the dreams about?"

A chill shot through Mara as she remembered. "Something was chasing me and I tried to run but I couldn't get away."

"A chase dream sounds pretty ordinary."

"The details were unusual." Again, she felt defensive. She closed her eyes for a moment, summoning memories. "The ground seemed to pound, and it was so hot, my feet burned. I think they were bare. I heard this loud, harsh breathing. Something huge and terrible blocked out the sun, but I could hardly move. I knew I was going to die."

She took a deep breath. Even now, after years of therapy, the imagery bothered her—a great lethal shadow. She'd concluded that the dream must have represented some deep level of anxiety, but she'd never figured out the cause.

Silent, Luke kept his eyes on the road.

"There's nothing in Kisi mysticism to interpret a dream like that?" she asked hopefully.

"Nightmares may be nothing but nightmares. You'd have to ask my grandmother if you wanted to know if there was anything more to a particular problem. She's the expert."

"You must have some expertise with dreams—you were in mine," Mara pointed out.

He glanced at her assessingly.

"Or I was in your dream," she amended, the sensual longings she'd felt then suddenly reclaiming her now. "However you choose to take it."

"I don't want to argue about that dream. I'd rather replay the footage for pure enjoyment."

Damn. And she'd had to bring it up again. Footage instantly replaying for her at the suggestion, Mara felt the same anticipation, the same dread....

She squirmed with discomfort.

And then changed the subject. "I used to draw my nightmares as a child. I thought putting them on paper would magically take them out of my mind."

"And did it work?"

"Sometimes. The drawings still scared me, abstract though they were. At least I could crumple them up and throw them away." She absently rubbed a finger along the edge of the window, gazing at a rocky red outcropping as they passed. "I think the whole process—doing the drawings, and wishing I could understand the nightmares in the first place—led me into art therapy."

"You studied the subject?"

"I worked in the field. I have a degree."

"So how come you're managing an art gallery now? Did you get laid off?"

"I quit." And she wasn't about to share why with Luke. Instead, she turned the conversation around to him. "Do you find painting therapeutic?"

When he didn't immediately answer her, she figured she'd hit one of his sore spots. He obviously had far more than she. And Luke was too reclusive and hostile to be open about much of anything.

That's why she was surprised when he admitted, "I *have* to paint."

"It's a compulsion?"

"Something like that."

"And you portray imagery from your dreams." As he'd already acknowledged.

"From some of my dreams. If I had a choice, I'd paint *instead* of dreaming a lot of the time." Again, the black, unrelenting gaze before he turned back to the road.

Luke wouldn't admit it but he must truly have horrific nightmares. Mara could empathize, though he was also entitled to his secrets. But as the Jeep climbed to higher terrain, clinging to narrow curves etched into the sides of steep hills, Mara found herself wanting to help him. She hated seeing anyone in psychological pain.

"Maybe your nightmares would be alleviated if you painted them," she suggested.

"If my bad dreams ended up on canvas, they wouldn't be hanging in anybody's gallery," he said tightly. "People would take one look and run away."

His tone chilled her. The paintings he did finish were haunting enough.

She stared out the window, recognizing the familiar crest of a mountain range not far from the Kisi pueblo. They would be arriving soon.

And she'd finally hear about Kisi mysticism.

Kisi dreamwalking.

Was the latter a type of lucid—or awake—dreaming, a state over which a person might exercise some control whether awake or asleep? Mara realized that was what she hoped to find out, prayed to learn herself by coming out here. So why hadn't Luke taken advantage of his obvious ability?

"Doesn't dreamwalking help you deal with nightmares?" she asked. "Can't you react in your dreams, make decisions, do what you want?"

His hard mouth softened, the corners turning up into a crooked smile. His sidelong glance raked over her. "If I could have done what I wanted with you last night, we would have both woken up a hell of a lot more relaxed this morning."

Her face grew warm as she thought about the lovemaking her dream-self had interrupted. The lovemaking part of her wanted to finish. She should have known better. Luke liked to intimidate her and he'd use any weapon that was handy, including his own sexual appeal.

Well, she could intimidate right back. "I did what *I* wanted to in the dream—told you to get lost."

Actually, she'd asked the dream-Luke to wait and he'd faded away. But the real man didn't disagree.

Despite herself, Mara felt the same inexplicable sadness as when they'd parted in the dream. Though she knew she should feel some sense of triumph. She already *could* exercise some control.

If talking to Isabel Joshevama could add to that, help her understand, reduce her fears, she'd feel as if she had a new lease on life. Nothing would throw her, not even the disturbing attraction she felt for the spooky man beside her.

Isabel motioned for Mara to take a seat when Luke led her into the narrow room directly off the kitchen.

Besides the two comfortable chairs arranged beneath a high, thick-silled window, the room was furnished simply—some wreaths of dried corn decorated the opposite wall, beneath which sat a single bed. At its foot stood a wooden chest, and beyond that a small draped table on which perched a kachina. A shaft of light from the window bathed the small figure, which seemed to be a serpent sprouting glimmering feathers.

Unusual. Mara had seen eagle kachinas and owls, wolves and other animal spirits portrayed as tiny dancing figures wearing sacred masks. But a serpent? She stared, prickles rising on her arms.

"You have entered my room, just as you entered my dreaming place. This time you were invited."

Mara turned her attention to the elderly woman, her curiosity and sense of triumph quickly fading into the awe she'd felt upon first learning that anyone could enter others' dreams. Isabel's words puzzled her. She glanced at Luke, a strong silent presence as he lounged against the wall near her chair.

"It was your grandson's dream, wasn't it? Not yours."

"I'm speaking of the night before last, when you approached me, hiding your face."

Mara was startled, then stunned. "You?" She'd had two dreamwalking experiences? "But the Indian woman in my dream was younger—"

"Because that is the way I still see myself in my visions. I'm strong, vital, not a blind old woman."

Mara could hardly believe it. Had Luke known? And why hadn't he told her? "How can it be?"

"Yes, how indeed? Where did you learn dream-walking?"

"I—I didn't learn it."

Isabel frowned. "You had no training?"

"I never even heard of dreamwalking...until Luke mentioned it today."

Isabel turned her face in Luke's direction. "Why did you explain anything, Stormdancer? I asked you to bring this woman to the pueblo, not give her any ideas."

Stormdancer?

"She wouldn't have come otherwise." Luke straightened, folding his arms across his chest. "And they have laws about carrying women off by force. I didn't think you'd want to see me end up in jail."

Emotions awhirl, Mara was angry. "Why shouldn't Luke explain a few things?" He could have stood to explain more. "He tried to hypnotize me."

Isabel raised her brows.

"Voice control, Grandmother," Luke explained. "But it didn't work. You know I'm not that skilled."

Mara's irritation grew. "Intimidation won't work. I came here of my own accord. I never meant any harm," she insisted. "I was just as shocked as you by the dreams I've been having, practically scared out of my wits."

Luke cut in, "You don't have to worry, Grand-mother, she's not a witch."

"A witch? How ridiculous." Though Mara herself had had momentary doubts about evil when she and Luke had talked in her condo. But she'd never stud-ied any sort of magic. "If anyone's practicing sor-cery, it's the Kisi, not me."

"The only sorcery I practice is healing the sick or seeking wisdom from spirits or ancestors. Or trying to protect my people," Isabel added.

Fascinating. "But let's get back to the dreamwalking. That's why I'm here. If you can go into more detail, maybe I can figure out how I managed to do it." If dreamwalking were like meditation, there might be buzzwords or specific images on which to concentrate. The latter she could have picked up through Luke's art.

When Isabel seemed to hesitate, Luke reiterated, "She's not evil."

Isabel leaned forward to slip a hand over hers. The Indian woman's touch was light, her flesh warm and dry, the bones inside it fragile. Was she testing vibrations or something? Mara was certain she felt a slight tingle of energy before the older woman slipped her hand away and sat back in her chair.

"Luke is right. You are not evil. Dreamseeking and dreamwalking are gifts handed down from one wise Kisi to the next," Isabel explained. "No one knows where they came from or when they began. Dreamseeking is the act of searching for a vision or a dream, either within yourself or someone else. Dreamwalking is actually entering someone else's dreams."

Dreamseeking. Dreamwalking. Mara could barely control her eagerness. "How do you do it? Control it?"

"It is best and most powerful to have a sacred spot, a site you know so well, you can see it with your eyes closed—a dreaming place."

"A dreaming place." Mara glanced over at Luke and once more remembered the dream she'd shared from what should have been the privacy of her own bed. "I've never had anything like that." She ripped her gaze from his in an attempt to dispel her growing tension that Isabel would no doubt sense. "This dreamwalking process is used to heal people?"

"Or to harm them. But the Kisi have traditionally avoided training the weak or the selfish, people who might be tempted into practicing witchcraft. We are careful. Only the wise should be powerful."

Luke shifted in the doorway. "Grandmother is a *finished person,* a wisewoman."

"Or a corn priestess, if we still practiced the ceremonies. There are few elders left. Traditions are being forgotten." Isabel stroked the beaded necklace she wore. "Perhaps evil is being conjured. That's why I was concerned about your appearance in my vision. At first," she mused, "I thought you were the spirit of an ancient one, an ancestor who'd come to give me a message."

"You can talk to the spirits of ancestors?"

"From time to time. Or to much greater... if you know the names to call...."

Mara's eyes were drawn to the serpent kachina.

"That one is especially sacred." In spite of her blindness, Isabel seemed aware of exactly what attracted her visitor's attention. "The sacred spirits of animals and clouds and mountains are called upon when the Kisi are in great need."

"And they protect you?"

"Or we protect ourselves," said Luke. Appearing restless all of a sudden, he straightened. "I'm going out." He looked at Mara. "When I come back, I'll drive you to Santa Fe."

Mara watched as he disappeared into the shadows beyond the kitchen. She felt empty inside without him near.

"He should truly *be* Stormdancer, a storm-bringer priest," said Isabel, her tone disapproving.

Mara knew too little to ask why Luke couldn't or wouldn't take up the calling. "A storm-bringer?"

"He should be able to call the rain and lightning. If necessary, send fireballs at enemies."

"Pretty powerful." But could she really believe it? Mara wondered. Dreams were one thing, fireballs another.

"Any kind of Kisi sorcery can be powerful," said Isabel, leaning forward again, making a sweeping gesture. "We can help plants grow, control animals and sometimes people for short periods of time. We can create illusions in both real life and dreams."

"Dreams are what interest me." What she'd already experienced was sorcery enough for Mara.

Isabel folded her hands in her lap and sat back. "But you do not know how you came to dreamwalk, and I'm afraid I've shared all that I can . . . with an outsider."

Disappointment, as well as a distinct feeling of rejection engulfed Mara. "You can't tell me anything else? I hoped to get some insight. Do you think I might be psychic? Is that what it could be?"

"Why should you turn your psychic abilities to us? Are you absolutely sure that you don't have one drop of Kisi blood?"

Mara didn't hesitate. "I'm certain. My mother traced our family tree—there were no Native Americans in it."

"And you don't think that someone else could have sent you into my dreaming place."

"Sent me?"

"Ordered you to do his or her bidding."

Mara hadn't even considered that. But she thought about the way she'd asked Luke to wait, effectively banishing him from her dream, about how she'd resisted his trick with the voice command today. Furthermore, she realized she'd been able to disappear when Isabel had shouted in her face.

"I don't think anyone exercises control over me." And she knew she was speaking the truth, felt it in her bones. "For some reason, somehow, I did what I did by myself."

Isabel nodded, her hands remaining folded, a thoughtful expression on her elegant aging face. "I must order you to stay out of my dreams from now on."

Again the feeling of rejection. And hurt. Mara swallowed. She was being shut out. "I hope I can oblige—I had nothing to say about it in the first place." No one controlled her, but surely it was also obvious she couldn't quite control herself.

"My visions are sacred to the Kisi. They are not for strangers. Do not tell anyone else about them," Isabel added.

"If I did, people would think I was crazy."

Isabel placed her hands on the arms of her chair to rise. "Our talk is finished." She gestured toward the door. "Now I would like you to meet someone else— my friend and fellow elder, Rebecca Harvier. Onida is serving refreshments outside again. We can join them for tea."

Tea? Mara hardly felt in the mood for a seat on the patio for refreshments. She wanted to find Luke, to demand he tell her more despite his grandmother's wishes. But in the end, she did the polite thing and agreed.

Mara could tell Onida was puzzled by her second visit, but the woman acted as gracious and friendly as she had the day before. Rebecca Harvier, a plump, gray-haired lady in her sixties, stared suspiciously at Mara from behind plastic-rimmed bifocals as she worked on a crocheted afghan.

Frustrated and hardly enlightened, Mara nevertheless tried to make small talk. "How pretty," she told Rebecca, admiring the afghan. "I like the desert colors—red and sand and turquoise. I used to crochet myself."

Rebecca seemed to relax a little and took a cookie. "I'm making this for my granddaughter. She's going to the University of New Mexico in Albuquerque."

"How nice. What's she majoring in?"

"Economics."

"Not an easy subject." Mara took a sip of tea.

Rebecca smiled, warming up. With a pleasant, ordinary face and multiple laugh lines crinkling out from her eyes, she seemed far less formidable than Isabel. "Ginnie is as smart as she is pretty. Only one more year to go of college. She'll be the first graduate in our family."

"I bet you're proud of her," Mara said sincerely, having come from a blue-collar family and a moderate income level herself. "I was the first in mine."

"Luke went to college in Arizona," Onida put in. "He took some art classes...but he didn't graduate."

"Where is Luke?" asked Isabel from the opposite side of the table.

Onida waved. "I saw him walking toward the community center. Maybe he's working on the murals."

The murals? Mara had thought he was planning on coming right back to the house for the return drive to Santa Fe. She was getting anxious. "It's getting late," she said, frowning at her watch. "I really should be going. Where's the community center, anyway? I'll find Luke."

After getting proper directions, she thanked the women and left, slipping her sweater over her shoulders. The afternoon had worn on and the air was growing cool. The sun blazed deep gold as it sped to the west, and the mountains darkened to blue-violet.

Confusion over her dreamwalking returned, and Mara felt too distracted to fully enjoy the natural beauty. She might as well have been walking through one of her dreams.

Striding past Tom Chalas's store, she noticed a crude metal sculpture sitting out behind it—the one that resembled an enslaved figure. She wondered if Tom had ever thought about apprenticing with another more successful sculptor. Perhaps doing so would help him.

Pondering that, she nearly missed the community center, a larger cinder block building set some yards beyond the store. Only a bulletin board in front of the building caught her eye with its fluttering flyers and notices.

As Mara turned, she thought she heard a skittering sound. Footsteps on gravel? Uncomfortable, she had the oddest feeling that someone was watching her....

She beat a path to the community center. It had a set of double doors and several windows with curtains, all of which were drawn. Going inside, she let her eyes adjust to sudden dimness. Surely the lack of lights meant no one was holding a meeting now. Luke also wasn't working on the murals. When she found the light switch, Mara caught sight of the wall paintings on the far side of the building's empty central room.

She gravitated across the linoleum floor as if drawn by a magnet, skirting chairs and circling a long table.

Spectacular. Surrounded by borders of traditional abstract designs and featuring the same haunting landscapes as Luke's usual paintings, the first mural depicted small figures of the gods or spirits climbing up from the underworld. The others were obviously meant to continue with the history and legends of the Kisi.

For the murals weren't finished. Against stunning mountain scenery and a shining sky, a sacred masked dance took place in one painting—figures swaying about a vivid blazing fire that seemed to have a life of its own. In the next, a pueblo had been sketched into the side of a cliff.

Something about the cliff dwelling looked familiar. Because it resembled Mesa Verde, an Anasazi ruin farther north in Colorado? From reading a history of the region, Mara knew the Kisi had rebuilt and lived in an old Anasazi site, which was where they had taken refuge at the time of the Spanish massacre. After that, the pueblo had become ruins again. It was located in a remote area of the Kisi reservation, off-limits for tourists.

Mara stood on tiptoe, trying to get a better look. The sketchy walls of the pueblo were familiar, yet nebulous as smoke—

Bam.

She started at the sound of the door slamming, then whipped around to see two Indians staring at her, one of them the bad-tempered, heavyset man she'd encountered in Chalas's store the day before. Charlie Mahooty. He plodded toward her, his gait unsteady.

"This center isn't open to tourists."

"I'm not a tourist. I came here with Lucas Naha."

But Mahooty came closer, his tall, stoop-shouldered companion on his heels. Both men wore unfriendly expressions and had alcohol on their breaths. The substance couldn't legally be sold on the reservation, but they'd gotten it somewhere.

"I don't care who you are to Naha," said Mahooty, poking at her arm, making her step back. "It's ten dollars to get onto the pueblo and thirty-five to look at these murals."

"Forty-five dollars?" Mara knew New Mexico pueblos often charged visitors for all sorts of things, but she'd already said she wasn't a tourist.

"Fork over the cash, lady. You don't want to spend the night locked up, do you?"

"You can't be serious."

"I'm real serious."

And belligerent looking, she thought. "I told you I know Lucas Naha. He brought me here today. If you talk to his grandmother—"

"I don't have to talk to anybody. I'm Charlie Mahooty, the governor of this place. I don't give a damn about Naha."

"And I don't give a damn about you, Mahooty," said Luke, suddenly appearing as if out of nowhere. "Leave the woman alone."

With a snarl, Mahooty plunged toward him.

CHAPTER FIVE

"**Y**ou're drunk." Expression cold, Luke easily side-stepped the shorter man, who charged, missed, then came at him again.

Mara huddled against the wall, wondering if she should take some sort of action. But Luke seemed to have things covered. When Mahooty threw a wild punch, he feinted and pushed his attacker backward so hard, the man stumbled and fell into a chair.

"You can't treat the governor like that," said Mahooty's companion. "I'm arresting you."

Luke made a menacing move, his jaw hard. "Yeah, Delgado? Go ahead—give me an excuse to rearrange your face for you."

Luke's intensity made his anger seem far more powerful than the simple belligerence of the other two men. Obviously rattled, Mahooty's pal backed away, running into a couple of chairs before he beat a retreat for the door.

Luke then concentrated on Mahooty, looming over him to take hold of his shirtfront. Though the older man was heavier and inebriated enough to be deadweight, Luke shook him like a rat.

"Don't you ever threaten me or mine, Mahooty!" Fury obviously growing, Luke resembled a predator about to strike a fatal blow. His hands moved from the shirtfront to Mahooty's throat. "So help me, I'll tear your head off. I'll—"

"Luke!"

He glanced up, releasing Mahooty. The man fell back into the chair, head lolling. Perhaps he'd passed out.

"Please." Mara touched Luke lightly. "You don't really want to harm him, do you?"

Luke gazed down at Mahooty with disgust. "Yeah, I want to harm him—but I won't."

"He's drunk. He doesn't know what he's doing. Why don't you let him sleep it off? You said you'd drive me back to Santa Fe."

Luke muttered something unintelligible, but at least he turned away. Mara sighed with relief as they walked toward the door. When it opened just as they were ready to exit the building, she wondered if it was Delgado returning.

Instead, Tom Chalas poked his head inside. "Something going on here?"

"Nothing you'd be interested in," Luke told him.

Chalas backed away, holding the door open to allow them passage. As Mara brushed past, he nodded a tight greeting, his expression understandably puzzled. Having seen her earlier at the gallery, he probably wondered what she was doing at the Kisi pueblo. But then, she did have a business association with Luke and might be friends with him, too.

She almost smiled, thinking about the latter. Then she remembered Luke telling Mahooty not to threaten "me or mine." Did he consider her *his?*

The idea titillated her.

It was all she could do to keep the idea at bay as Luke helped her into the Jeep Comanche, his hand warm and brash on her arm. As he let go, the backs of his fingers brushed the side of her breast. He stood there a second, his gaze meshing with hers, his expression as intense as it had been when he'd dealt with the bully. As he rounded the vehicle, she shook off her very physical and all-too-familiar reaction to him.

And as he started the Jeep, she told herself that Luke's primary inclination hadn't been to protect her from Mahooty. More likely the situation had merely triggered his fiery anger. He always seemed to be sizzling beneath the surface. She didn't bring up the fight at all until they were a half hour down the highway and nearing the outskirts of Santa Fe. By that time, she'd begun to consider the repercussions.

"Will you really be arrested when you go back to the pueblo?" she asked. "Onida said that Mahooty was elected governor today."

"I won't be arrested. Mahooty knows he was out of line."

Personally, she didn't think the man should serve as any sort of leader. "It doesn't look too good, does it, the governor being drunk?"

"He and his cronies were probably celebrating."

"The man with Mahooty, was he tribal police?" she asked. "He was drunk, too. Isn't that rather dangerous?"

"He was off duty."

And hadn't been toting a gun, thank God. "So being off duty makes drunkenness okay? Do the people of the Kisi pueblo really want men like that to have authority?"

Luke's glance slid sideways. "How many more questions you got—forty...a thousand?"

She ignored his sarcasm. "I can't help being curious, as well as concerned. I don't like people who bully their way into positions of power." Which Rebecca had indicated Mahooty had done during their tea. "How could you let that happen?"

"How could *I* let it happen? I stay out of the pueblo's business."

"Even though your grandmother and mother are worried?"

This time, Luke gave her a dirty look. "You came out to the pueblo to talk about dreamwalking, not get involved with how it's run."

Dreamwalking? The incident at the community center had temporarily driven the subject from her mind, but now it brought a new slant.

"Your grandmother is a wisewoman. Can't she stop a tyrant like Mahooty?"

"She's always concerned herself with healing and wisdom. She's never practiced any other sort of sorcery. And she would never try...unless what's left of the Kisi people begged her to do it, I suppose. Or her family needed protection."

"The Kisi respect her."

"Some of them."

"Only some? A person who can dreamwalk?"

"Not everyone thinks visions are important, that they serve a practical purpose." He added, "Dreamwalking can't get you a job."

Perhaps not, but it meant a lot to her. "I think the whole concept is positively miraculous."

Her problems with nightmares hadn't been solved, but that dreamwalking existed at all made her think there actually could be a solution.

As she thought about that, a weight seemed to lift from her heart, a burden she'd been carrying for a long time. The interview with Isabel had been frustrating, and the Indian woman hadn't even touched on her deepest questions, but she had learned some incredible things.

She stared out at the desert, where dusk crept down from the foothills, and gazed at the world through new eyes. Far more was possible than she'd ever believed.

Though there are possibilities for evil, as well as good, a little voice whispered inside her head.

Another, different worry now pressed her. "All Kisi can't dreamwalk, right? Your grandmother said only the wise were trained. Charlie Mahooty doesn't have any powers."

"I hope not."

But she noticed Luke hadn't denied it.

"Mahooty talks about sorcery," Luke went on. "But he uses the subject to intimidate other Indians. He's been promising to protect the Kisi. That's why they elected him."

"Protect the Kisi from what?"

"Whatever."

Obviously, he didn't want to say. Uneasy, she gazed out the window again, the landscape now completely dark. "I'm sure no one in your family voted for Mahooty. And Rebecca certainly doesn't like him."

"He's not respectful of elders."

Mara remembered that Isabel had called Rebecca an elder. "Is Rebecca a wisewoman like your grandmother?"

"Uh-huh."

"Meaning she can dreamwalk?"

"She was trained."

Mara was surprised. "I would never guess—she appears to be a normal, comfortable sort of grandmother." As opposed to Isabel, who radiated power. "Does your mother dreamwalk?" she probed.

"She didn't have the calling, the concentration. Either you do or you don't."

Concentration. Now, Luke had plenty of that. Otherwise, he wouldn't be able to spend so many hours by himself painting. And he certainly had power. Mara swore she could feel it emanating from him as they drove along, two souls confined to the isolation of the vehicle, night hemming them in.

It was Luke's power that made his anger so frightening. Of which Mahooty was surely aware. He'd looked plenty scared before he'd passed out.

Still Mara had doubts. "Since Mahooty hates you and has no respect for Isabel, do you really feel safe staying out at the pueblo?"

"Grandmother can protect her family if she has to."

"And what about you?"

"You saw me put Mahooty in his place."

"With your physical strength." She plunged right in, knowing she might offend him. "How come you won't try to develop your other skills, your mental abilities?" Which his grandmother had implied he wasn't making use of. "Surely Isabel can help you combat the nightmares—"

"You don't know beans about my nightmares," he snapped.

He *was* offended.

"And no one can help me," he added bluntly, bitterly, effectively cutting her off.

She didn't know what else to say. Either his dreams were more horrifying than any she'd ever experienced or he was more frightened than she was at some deep level. Further, he obviously had no hope for his situation ever getting any better.

Mara was determined not to feel so hopeless herself. Especially now that she no longer feared she was going crazy, now that she realized she'd actually taken some sort of action in her dreams. After all, she'd refused Luke's advances and had run away from Isabel. That was something.

She would simply trust that there would be more, that she could conquer her terrors, that she would be able to handle herself in bizarre, even threatening situations. She reassured herself of that over and over as they drove on silently, the final miles slipping by.

Meanwhile, the moon came up and the sky exploded with stars. Lights bloomed at ground level as the Jeep topped a hill overlooking Santa Fe.

As they approached town, Luke still made no effort to converse. But at least he'd responded when Mara had spoken to him, hadn't snapped at her too badly during the ride. He'd been relatively personable on the trip out, as well.

Why? Was their relationship changing?

Reflecting on that, Mara realized she felt some sort of bond with Luke. It was strange, inexplicable, if similar to her connection with *Lightning Over Red*

Mesa. The painting spooked her too much to hang it in the main room, but she wanted it, anyway. *Lightning* was a haunting painting, just as Luke was a haunting man.

A *haunted* man, she felt in her gut, glancing toward him, at his powerful hands on the steering wheel. She had seen those hands creating incredible art and had also seen them go for Charlie Mahooty's throat.

What demons drove Luke Naha? Surely more than nightmares. Had something chilling happened in his past? His behavior and attitude bespoke mysteries that needed to be solved.

Mysteries. Mara wondered where Luke had gone for that hour or so, while Onida had thought he'd been working on his murals. Whose footsteps had scrabbled on the gravel behind her? Who had been watching her? Luke had appeared in the community center not much later, and suddenly, as if out of nowhere.

But what reason did he have to sneak about?

Dismissing her suspicions, she saw they'd reached the city limits. Streetlights flooded the road. Luke kept driving, didn't bother to ask where her building was. But he obviously remembered the address, since he made the correct turns, pulling the Jeep up in front of the condo complex minutes later.

For some reason, she felt hesitant to leave his company.

"Afraid of something? I can walk you to the door, if you want."

She was only half joking when she said, "And ruin your mystique? That would be far too polite."

He cut the engine and got out when she did. As they strolled down the cement walk, she felt his presence as palpable warmth. But who wouldn't be aware of such a lean, muscular body, such a graceful, gliding walk?

The hands that created paintings and threatened Mahooty had also held her, stroked her nearly mad with passion. Just thinking about that made desire stir within her. Luke Naha was mysterious and powerful, with or without sorcery. He had cast his own sort of dark spell on her.

For why else did she turn to face him when they reached her door? Why else did she forget about searching for her keys? Why else did she lift her face up to him expectantly?

Their eyes met for a moment before he slid his arms about her possessively. Then he covered her mouth with warm, searching lips.

She wasn't surprised. She wouldn't object that he was reneging on his promise not to touch her. With the two of them, it always seemed to come down to this.

They kissed deeply, sweetly. He slipped a hand beneath her sweater and ran his fingers up the length of her spine. She arched, tingling, feeling every finger through the fabric of her blouse. Her arms slid about him of their own accord, and she luxuriated in the play of muscles across his back.

Her nipples tightened as they nestled against his hard chest. He rubbed her against him, then took hold of her waist to walk her backward into the shadows near the building's doorway. When she ran her fingers through his hair, she loosened the cord that tied it back. It felt much softer than she'd imagined.

He leaned her against the adobe wall, cupping a breast and brushing his thumb across the sensitive crest. She nearly cried out. It seemed only natural when he slid a knee between her legs and anchored himself against her. He tilted his pelvis so she could better feel the hard proof of his desire. Heat rising from her lower belly, she rocked her hips against him, moaning.

She wanted to protest when he suddenly lifted his head.

"Let's head upstairs . . . to bed."

His blunt words broke the spell. Mara opened her eyes, felt her blood singing through her veins, her heart beating jaggedly. Even so, she fought for her breath, her wits, fought to distance herself from the man looming over her.

What was she doing? She didn't know Luke Naha well enough to make love with him. And something much deeper bothered her . . . she wasn't certain she could trust him.

"I don't think going to bed is a good idea," she said breathlessly.

He scowled. "It's a perfect idea. You want me, I want you."

"But that's only lust."

"What? Don't want to mess up your pretty bedroom?" he asked huskily. "We can use my truck."

How earthy, urgent. And in part, a turn-on. She called on all her strength to deny her own desires.

"No, Luke."

He made a sound of disgust, releasing her so suddenly, she stumbled and almost fell. "You're driving me crazy, woman."

Then he stalked off.

Reminded of the way he'd left her in the dream, she stood there watching him start the Jeep. This time, she didn't call him back. With a squeal of tires, he zoomed off. Red taillights winked like animal eyes, then were swallowed up by darkness.

So she was driving Luke crazy. Well, he drove her crazy, too... and, for once, that word had little to do with the state of her mental health.

The black of midnight mirrored his emotions as he cruised down the Fitzgerald woman's street. He stopped his vehicle and stared up at the top floor of her building, noting the height of the balcony fronting her apartment. Behind the wrought iron, the glass doors glowed with dim light.

Was the bitch afraid to sleep in the dark? He wished he could get inside her head and really make her scream.

But that would be difficult and time-consuming when he had so many other things to do. Not to mention that he wasn't certain how his techniques would affect the mind of a non-Indian. He would have to settle for trying to frighten the woman on the physical plane.

He got out, taking the bag from behind his seat. The cool air hit him full in the face. He had to pause, feeling dizzy, swallowing nausea. He'd overindulged himself. He took a deep breath to combat his swirling vision, fighting to maintain control. When the ground stopped spinning, he crept carefully into the shadows of some low bushes.

He positioned himself beneath the balcony and the lit door, then took the bloody rawhide doll out of his bag.

Grasping the repulsive thing about its neck, he imagined he had hold of *her*. He hated the nose-in-the-air bitch, despised her so much it felt like he'd known her for a long, long time. The Yaqui had said she was bad medicine, had read it in the entrails of the chicken they'd slaughtered earlier.

She could examine the message for herself . . . if she knew entrails.

Sniggering, he tightened the cord around the doll, whose belly had been slit to hold the chicken's stinking, bloody guts. Then he made sure that the bits of blue and brown yarn he'd collected from her sweater were firmly stuck in place with cactus spines.

"Pain!" he muttered, pushing a spine deeper into the doll's head. "Fear!" He hoped she'd suffer double doses of both.

Though there'd be far worse to come if she wasn't smart enough to stay away from the Kisi reservation, if not leave the state entirely.

Carefully aiming the doll at the balcony, he heard a set of dual thuds as it hit the glass and plopped down onto the balcony floor. He hoped the blood had splattered everywhere.

And that the noise had awakened her. Wanting to enjoy her terror, he waited a few minutes to see if she'd appear.

When she didn't, he swore softly but turned away, heading back for the truck. The night wouldn't last forever. He needed to focus all his energy, to conjure up an ancient and elemental power. . . .

Mara woke so suddenly, she nearly jumped off the couch.

The logs in the kiva fireplace crackled.

Head pounding, feeling disoriented, she sat straight up and gazed about the living room. Down the hall, light spilled out from the bathroom. The hands of the clock sitting on her bookshelf stood at one o'clock.

Everything seemed quiet. Nothing was wrong.

Except for her headache.

She got up and stumbled across the living room. She simply hadn't been able to crawl into her bed or immerse herself in complete darkness tonight. That would have been asking for dreams...from which she badly needed a rest.

Had she dreamed, anyway? Was that what had startled her awake? Or had there been some sort of unusual noise?

She seemed to remember hearing something, but perhaps it had only been the beat of her throbbing head.

Turning on the faucet in the kitchen, she filled a glass with water and took some aspirin. The familiar task made her feel a little more secure.

But she continued to glance about as she walked down the hall and turned on the overhead light in the bedroom.

Empty. Safe.

Though she wished she weren't alone.

Luke coming to mind whether she bid him or no, she went back to the living room and heaped more wood on the fire.

For protection against the night?

She slid her eyes from the fire to the dark rectangle of the room's double glass doors, wondering if she should check the lock. Even though she'd already done so, at least twice before going to sleep.

She decided she wouldn't, didn't want to look any farther than her own home and hearth.

She poked the wood in the fireplace until flames leapt and crackled. Gold-orange heat.

Fire.

Like the blaze that always seemed to be sizzling within Luke.

Unfortunately, an image so unsettling, it didn't make her want to go back to sleep.

Fire!

Smoke billowed around him, filled his nostrils, seared his eyes. Fighting pain, he tried to find a way out, only to be stopped dead by crashing vigas. The whole place was being eaten alive!

Sparks flew, bright incendiaries that landed, flared and roared into dancing flames.

Flames that matched his burning anger.

His fury simmered, seethed ... until he spotted the shadow slipping into the darkness beyond the fire. With shock, he realized it was mocking him, laughing at him, that it wished him to die....

Evil!

Malevolence far worse than any fire.

Swallowing his fear, he roared out a war cry, then swore, even as more burning beams came crashing down about his ears....

"Damn you! Damn..." Luke woke with a start, his sheet, blankets and pillows all thrown to the floor.

Another nightmare.

He hadn't had one for a while. And he figured this dream must have been brought about by sexual frustration, combined with the beers and spicy tortilla chips he'd guzzled instead of eating supper. He rarely drank alcohol and now had an upset stomach.

Cursing a blue streak, he swung his legs over the side of the bed and sat up. That's when he remembered the shadow in the dream—a new and sinister element— and heard the commotion outside.

Someone yelled and banged a door. Feet pounded past the house.

What the hell?

Leaping up, he grabbed for his jeans, then realized he was already wearing them. He bolted for the bedroom door, where he came face-to-face with Onida.

She clutched her robe, very upset. "There's a fire, Luke!"

"Here?"

"No, but it may be someone else's home. Oh my God!"

Luke didn't bother to speculate on the site. Patting his mother's shoulder, he gently moved her aside. Then he rushed out the door.

Fire!

He could smell it on the wind, acrid, deadly. It seemed to be coming from the vicinity of Chalas's store and the community center.

He ran, his bare feet slapping the cold, hard ground. Paying no attention to sharp rocks, he kept his eyes on the knot of people gathering up ahead.

As he approached, he saw that the pueblo's firefighting unit had a hose snaking into the community center. Black smoke billowed out.

At least it hadn't been anyone's house. No one's life was in danger. Taking a breath of relief, he came to a stop beside a woman with two children clinging to her legs.

"What happened?"

The woman glanced up at Luke. "I don't know. The building is burning inside."

"Electrical short, I bet," said someone else standing nearby.

"Short, my eye," said yet another bystander, a middle-aged woman with her hair in braids. "It was witchcraft."

Witchcraft?

His skin crawling, Luke stared at the woman.

She needed no urging to go on. "There was this fiery ball and it floated right through the door...a witchlight."

"You saw it?" Luke asked.

"Mattie Stolla told me. She was standing at her kitchen window. There's terrible evil about."

Or misguided sorcery.

Ignoring that the woman was staring at him like he was responsible, Luke moved off.

Witchlight? A fireball?

Feeling sick, he approached the fire fighters, offering them a hand. Several worried that the water pressure from the pueblo's main pump would run out.

But ten minutes later, Mahooty's pal Delgado emerged from the building, his T-shirt black with smoke and grime. "We got it, boys."

The man had slept off his drunkenness, Luke noted. "Fire's out?"

Delgado gazed at him speculatively. "Yeah, only ruined a couple of interior walls." Then he smiled as he realized who he was talking to. "Your murals are gone, Naha. Nothing we could do."

The murals.

Luke didn't react. In truth, he didn't feel that bad, though he'd put in a lot of work at the center, original paintings that could never quite be recreated.

At least no lives had been lost.

Luke could tell the other men were surprised when he went to work, helping them with the cleanup.

But his relief was short-lived. His mind roiled—a fireball had destroyed the murals? He hadn't been angry about them for days and days.

He'd been angry with . . . Mara Fitzgerald.

Adrenaline zinging, he dropped what he was doing and took off, seeking the pay phone near Chalas's store. It had to be four o'clock in the morning, but he didn't care. Obtaining Mara's number from information, he punched in the digits. His concern grew as her phone rang and rang.

Finally she picked up, her voice husky, sleepy. "Hello?"

He let his breath out slowly in relief. Thank God, she was alive, hopefully safe.

"Hello? Who is this?" she said more insistently. "Damn it, I'm not in the mood for heavy breathing."

He wasn't afraid of her anger. It wasn't tainted by shadow or made of fire. "This is Luke. Go back to sleep."

"Luke . . ."

But he was already replacing the receiver.

Though he needed to talk.

Though he needed to confide in someone.

And whether he liked it or not, he knew it was going to have to be her.

CHAPTER SIX

When her alarm went off the next morning, Mara awoke bleary-eyed. She reached for the clock radio she'd brought from the bedroom and turned it off. Then she rose carefully, her head still pounding. Adding to that, her neck felt as if it had been twisted, then frozen into position. She must have slept wrong on the unfamiliar couch, probably pinched a nerve.

Mara glanced at the clock—7:00 a.m. The last time she'd looked, the dial had announced 4:30. That had been after she'd managed to settle down and get over the embarrassment of phoning Luke right back, only to reach Onida. Mara had hung up without identifying herself, a trick she'd never pulled before in her life.

Once again wondering where the man had been calling from and why, she struggled into the robe she'd tossed into a chair and made her way to the kitchen. More aspirins. Then she dampened a tea towel with cold water and placed it on her forehead before returning to face the brilliance of the morning sun.

A shaft of bright light blazed through the sliding doors...and illuminated some rusty-colored smears on the glass. The doors hadn't been dirty yesterday. Frowning, Mara approached, undid the latch, then dropped the tea towel when she spotted the gruesome mess on the balcony.

Blood. Blood splattered the concrete floor and the outer adobe wall. A trail of thick blood mixed with entrails led to a disgusting lump lying near the wrought-iron bars.

Mara swallowed, fighting the desire to scream, the instinctive urge to vomit. Her pulse surged. Her flesh crawled.

But she had to get a closer look. Trembling, she pushed the door open farther and emerged into full sunlight.

Pulling up the hem of her robe, she stared down at what appeared to be a small figure made of rough hide. Its middle was slit and spewing more entrails. Cactus spines stuck out here and there.... But what drew her eye was some fuzz skewered by the spine piercing the doll's head. Brown and blue yarn. A tuft from her own sweater.

My God, was it some sort of voodoo doll?

She backed away, shivering.

Someone must have thrown it from the yard below. It had bounced off the glass doors with a thud...which was no doubt what had awakened her the night before.

But who would do something like this?

Luke?

Was that why he'd called in the wee hours, to see if she'd discovered his grisly surprise?

He must have been furious when she'd refused to go to bed with him.

More than furious. If this was his work, Luke Naha was far more than an angry man bothered by nightmares. He was seriously—possibly dangerously—troubled.

* * *

Even ammonia and scrubbing hadn't removed all the bloodstains on the balcony. Mara was late for work.

Her eyes puffy, her hair messily French braided when she hadn't had time to set it, the pants outfit she'd thrown on a little wrinkled, she knew she must look a sight.

But Felice made no comment as they worked together in the storeroom, deciding how to frame and display Luke's newest paintings.

Felice admired one of the pieces he'd dropped off at the gallery the day before. "I don't believe I've ever seen a cliff dwelling in Naha's work before."

Hardly enthusiastic, Mara merely nodded. She'd already noted the imagery in his murals.

"The effect is so ephemeral," Felice went on. "Like the pueblo's there but it's not, as if it could disappear in smoke."

A dabble of vivid red could be seen within the primitive building. The color reflected the land from which it had sprung—rugged, wild, as deep and red as ancient blood. Overhead, a cobalt sky seemed ready for an outburst of stars. The usual tiny figure stood at the bottom of the cliff, seeming to gaze upward. The whole effect was darker and even more eerie than the normal Naha painting, as if night were coming on.

Night. Mara shivered, then took the painting and turned its face toward the storeroom wall. She wished she could as easily forget the night before, the bizarre phone call, the token Luke had left for her.

When a customer came in, Felice hurried out to the gallery's sales area. Which gave Mara the chance to take a break and rub her sore neck. At least the aspirins had reduced her headache to a dull throb.

Felice returned to the storeroom when the customer left. She helped Mara carry *Sun Dog* into the storeroom and place it with the other four paintings. Represented by such a limited number of pieces, Luke would barely take up the main room. But that would have to do. And, at the moment, Mara hardly cared.

"What happened to the other paintings you were going to see at the reservation yesterday?"

Mara had forgotten she'd given that excuse. Now she had to lie a second time. "They're in progress. Naha just wanted me to see the direction he's taking. Hopefully, we'll still be able to get hold of a couple of them before the show."

"He must like you."

"As much as he likes anyone," Mara hedged. Felice had seen Luke embracing her in the office, but Mara had no intention of talking about their strange attraction. And she couldn't mention dreamwalking. "I got some insight into his work methods."

"Hmm, now you know this guy better than anyone else in Santa Fe. And was I surprised when I saw him," Felice added. "I never thought he'd be so good-looking." Then she waited expectantly, no doubt hoping her boss would mention something more personal.

Mara couldn't quite accommodate her. "Too bad his personality doesn't match his face."

"Meaning he's a jerk?"

"Unfortunately."

Or worse. Mara rubbed her aching neck again.

"You feeling okay?"

"I had some trouble sleeping."

"More nightmares?"

"Too much caffeine, I guess. I was restless."

Another fib.

Several minutes passed before Mara realized Felice might be able to add some insight to the situation. She tried to be indirect. "Do you know whether Indians in this area ever make little figures out of hide?"

"And stick cactus spines through them? Uh-huh. It's a superstitious thing—sort of an Indian curse doll."

"Like voodoo?"

"Similar." Felice's glance was curious. "Did you see one at the Kisi reservation?"

A curse doll. Unnerved, Mara managed to maintain a blank expression. "I heard about them, that they're sometimes filled with bloody entrails."

Felice made a face. "Yuk. Maybe entrails are for an especially powerful spell. I know that strands of the victim's hair or nail shavings are sometimes attached."

"Or pieces of clothing?" Like the tufts of yarn Luke could have found in his truck.

"That'd probably work, too."

"Surely a curse doesn't have any power over a person unless he believes in it." Though the headache that had come on last night—and still tormented her—made Mara wonder how much she believed about the Kisi.

Felice stared, obviously picking up on the tension. "Are you worried about some Indian getting mad and putting a curse on you? Like Lucas Naha? I thought you said he kind of likes you."

"True."

Mara changed the subject as they continued to work. She made notations while Felice measured the paintings. All the while she was sick inside, not only that any human being could have sent her such an angry message, but that it had undoubtedly been a man to whom she was so deeply attracted. A man with whom she'd shared a highly erotic dream.

Closing time approached quickly. Announcing she had a Friday-night date, Felice made haste to lock up. Mara went into her office and took out some long-overdue paperwork.

Slinging on her jacket, Felice stopped by, lounging in the doorway. "You know, I heard you can protect yourself and your home from evil magic by burying a little bag of powdered turquoise with some grains of corn near your doorstep."

Mara knew the other woman was only trying to be helpful, but the discussion had gone as far as she wanted. "That would be a little difficult, since my condo's on the second floor."

"How about hanging a bag over every entrance-way, then?"

Mara managed a wry smile. "Thanks for the suggestion—if I start fearing evil magic, I'll think about it."

Evil magic.

Sorcery? Isabel Joshevama also had reason to try to frighten her, Mara knew. The elderly woman had ordered her to stay out of her dreams. Maybe Isabel thought a hide doll would scare her into leaving Santa Fe.

Well, Mara wasn't budging, neither because Luke
sought to get even with her, nor because his grandmother wanted her out of the way. And she wasn't
hanging little bags of powdered turquoise around, either, even if she knew where to obtain the materials.

She tried to put everything out of her mind as she
attacked the paperwork for the next half hour. Unfortunately, her headache and fatigue soon made the
figures blur. Realizing overtime would be impossible,
she reluctantly got ready to leave. She'd simply have
to spare some hours tomorrow.

Outside, the sun prepared to set in red brilliance.
But there was plenty of clear light left to see by. The
summer air smelled fresh and sharp with the scent of
piñon pine. Mara felt the headache recede and her
muddled brain clear a bit. Not that she intended to do
anything more than head home, lock all the doors and
crawl into bed. She'd surely feel better tomorrow,
could work a few hours and be able to take Sunday off
entirely.

She looked forward to that. She needed time to mull
over what had happened, try to figure out what she
was going to do and if there was anywhere she could
find less-direct sources for information on Kisi magic
and dreamwalking.

She ambled down the street on which St. Francis
Cathedral stood, a landmark of Santa Fe. With its
magnificent round stained-glass window and squared-
off bell tower, the church was a beautiful sight. As
were the many other historical buildings she passed on
her way to and from the gallery every day. Though
traditional residents preferred to drive, Mara liked to
walk, enjoying a healthy six- or seven-block stroll.

Tonight the historical part of the city was busier than usual, with tourists seeking parking spots and Friday-night crowds chattering as they waited in front of popular restaurants. Guitar music wafted out from one establishment as Mara went by.

The music was lovely but her head demanded silence.

Which was why she decided to take her alternate route home. Several arroyos ran through the town, waterways for runoffs when too much snow melted off the surrounding mountains. One of the larger, deeper ditches passed by her condo complex, a shorter path as the crow flew.

Already appreciating the quieter atmosphere, she eased herself down the steep bank. Below, the earth rose high enough on either side to allow her to believe she was alone with nature. Long desert grass, a bit brown from lack of moisture, crunched beneath her booted feet. The snow runoff was over and Santa Fe could use a shower.

A few yards along, thinking of the wet northern California climate she somehow didn't miss, she heard soft skittering sounds that reminded her of raindrops.

But it wasn't raining.

Mara suddenly became alert. Something was moving along behind her. A stray cat or some small wild creature? She glanced over her shoulder to see a lithe form glide into a brushy copse of chamisa. The animal seemed larger than a rabbit or a cat.

A bit spooked, she ordered herself to relax and kept on walking. She was a little farther when she became aware of more sounds.

A scrabbling like claws on rocks.

Soft panting.

She stopped in her tracks and whipped around to get a better look. Several forms skulked off into the brush, definitely canine in shape. Coyotes? The animals did come into town once in a while, but people rarely saw them.

Perplexed, Mara nevertheless refused to worry. She'd heard tales about coyotes following hikers or horseback riders out of curiosity. The animals weren't dangerous.

Though being trailed felt very eerie.

She forged onward, walking a little faster. Her pant leg caught on some thorny branches, forcing her to stop and extricate herself. She heard more scrabbling sounds, then a soft yap.

Enough. Mara swiveled around again to face her pursuers.

This time she counted at least six or seven coyotes, more animals than the surrounding brush could hide. They froze, their grayish yellow pelts nearly blending with the growing dusk and shadows.

Chilled, she felt her heartbeat accelerate. Were the animals multiplying? And why were they following her?

She was damn well climbing out of the arroyo!

Thank goodness she'd sighted the concrete viaduct up ahead. It meant she was near her destination.

She glanced about, looking for the easiest way to climb, and found it some yards away, a barren spot with less of an incline. Striding forward, she stopped with a gasp when a very large coyote burst out from the shadows, cutting off her path.

The red sunset put a glitter into the animal's eyes and made its pale coat glow yellow.

Her heart was in her throat as she stepped forward and shook her fist. "Go away!"

The animal bared its teeth and growled.

Mara grew a bit panicky. This wasn't typical coyote behavior at all.

"Shoo!" she shouted. "Get out of here!"

Then she heard soft footfalls and glanced about to see that the rest of the animals seemed intent on surrounding her. They gazed at her expectantly, tongues lolling, jaws open.

Sorcery!

She remembered Isabel saying that sorcerers could control animals.

The big yellow coyote advanced toward her.

"Damn it, I said get out of here!"

At the same time, she stooped to grab some rocks. They were small but they could hurt, which she proved by throwing at the yellow beast. Yelping as the rock bounced off its side, it retreated, several companions following.

Mara relaxed slightly.

But then the big coyote wheeled and headed straight back toward her.

Hairs standing up on the back of her neck, she yelled at the top of her lungs and threw a rock as hard as she could. The missile thunked on the animal's head, and she thought she saw him fall. Then she was running, scrambling up the bank for all she was worth, slipping and sliding in her panic. Near the top, she pitched forward but managed to regain her feet.

She didn't see the man above on the walkway until she ran smack into him. Strong hands grasped her shoulders as she fought for her breath. Heart thudding against her chest, she stared up into a familiar, hard face.

"Luke!"

"Was that you doing all the yelling?"

Her adrenaline started zinging all over again, partly because of his nearness and partly because of renewed fear. If the coyotes had been conjured by sorcery, he was the only Kisi in the vicinity.

She punched at him. "Damn it, let go! You have a lot of nerve, you bastard!"

He released her with a scowl. "What the hell's the matter with you?"

"Coyotes!"

"You saw one?"

"What are you doing here, Luke?" Had he followed her from work? "Trying to exercise some more of your stupid witchcraft? Well, you can take your spells and go back to the reservation."

He could be faking his look of surprise. She gestured to the arroyo. "Don't pretend that you don't know what I'm talking about," she said, gesturing to the arroyo. "There were at least half a dozen coyotes down there and they weren't acting normal."

Peering over the edge of the viaduct, he barely paused before moving toward the barren slope she'd just climbed. The streetlights popped on the very moment he disappeared into the dusk, the pale gray of the arroyo deepening to opaque charcoal. Mara heard soft footfalls below.

Despite being in the midst of a small city, she seemed to stand alone in the shadow-filled twilight. The interval between day and night, a setting that made everything appear real and unreal at the same time.

But did she really believe in sorcery? Mara wondered. Could Luke—or anyone—control animals?

Niggling doubts couldn't stop her heart from starting to race all over again when she heard someone or something moving back up the slope. Instinctively, she backed away.

Luke suddenly reappeared.

He looked like a man, not a spell-wielding sorcerer. At least his eyes didn't glitter.

She halted, tried to get herself to settle down. She was safe...wasn't she?

He scowled. "You still freaked out? There's some prints down there but nothing else."

Prints. That meant the animals had actually existed. "The coyotes are gone?"

"Of course they're gone. You can find them anywhere in this state, but they never hurt anyone—"

Upset, she cut in. "They were stalking me, Luke. There was a big yellow one that bared his teeth. I don't need a lecture."

"A yellow coyote?"

"He tried to corner me and I hit him in the head with a rock." She tried to justify the accusations she'd hurled at him. "I couldn't help but think of sorcery—Isabel said some people could control animals."

"And you're assuming that someone is me?" He stepped closer.

But she refused to back up any more. She couldn't hide her anger, not after the last twelve hours. "Look, some creep left a bloody, disgusting hide doll on my balcony last night—full of entrails and stuck through with cactus spines and yarn from my sweater. Then I got the weird call from you at around four a.m. Were you checking up on your handiwork? Is that why you're here?"

A watchful, almost wary expression crossed his face. "Did you see someone leave the doll?"

She noted he wasn't trying to defend himself. "I didn't see anything. I heard a thud when something hit my balcony doors." At least, she thought that's what had awakened her.

"What time was that?"

She tried to remember, recalled the clock on the bookshelf. "One a.m."

"One." He nodded, for some reason looking oddly satisfied. "I was in my studio painting at that time."

But *she* wasn't satisfied. "So you say. But even if you have witnesses to prove otherwise, you could have sent someone else to carry out your orders."

"I like to work on my own."

Reluctantly, she nodded. Probably true. Somehow, as disgusting as it would be if Luke had been the one to send her the message, she would feel safer than she did now. She shuddered as she thought of some stranger stalking her.

"I'm not responsible for the coyotes, either," He said. "Besides, if I had that skill, if I wanted to use it against you, we wouldn't be standing here talking." He quirked a brow. "They would've gotten you."

A pleasant scene to imagine. And one that hardly alleviated the doubts she was trying to push aside. Her heart thudded in her breast as he stepped closer. His nearness engulfed her whole.

"My truck's down the street. Let's go."

Her nostrils filled with his unique scent—his maleness mixed with the tools of an artist. She could hardly breathe. "Go where?"

"A restaurant I know of. I'm hungry, and you could probably use some dinner, too."

Teetering on the edge of hysteria, she laughed. "Dinner?" Surely he wasn't trying to be friendly...or romantic. Though thinking about the latter possibility brought tingles of anticipation. "You're out of your mind."

"Aren't you hungry?"

She was still too upset to know. "I can't think about food now."

"Then have a stiff drink. You could stand one."

"It's a bit difficult for me to skip from sorcery to drinks or food."

"We can compromise. Cover sorcery while we eat."

He motioned toward his truck a second time. She noticed it was sitting in front of her building. There was an urgency about him—she sensed it—but he made no move to touch her. Could she trust him or not? Time cleared her head a bit. She'd gone out to the reservation and returned unharmed.

"I came to see you, to talk," he said, finally offering a reason for his presence. "I figured you'd come home eventually. If nothing else, we might as well finish up that conversation we could have had at four a.m. Something unusual happened."

Something unusual. An explanation for the phone call.

Despite herself, Mara was caught. Again.

Fascination warred with suspicion and won. A heady brew when mixed with the attraction between them. "All right. I'll come."

As they headed for his truck, she figured she wouldn't have been able to settle down, anyway. She would have sat around her apartment, nervous, staring at the walls, as she tried to understand what had happened.

Luke might be spooky, his actions mysterious, yet he still made her feel less alone.

CHAPTER SEVEN

"Where did you learn Kisi?" Luke asked as he and Mara relaxed over a plate of nachos at a traditional Mexican restaurant in an unfashionable part of town. He hated the new places with their fancy food and tourists.

"Kisi? What are you talking about?"

"I heard you shout 'Beware' in that language when I was walking along the arroyo."

"I don't know anything but English. I was only yelling."

Though Luke wasn't an expert himself, he recognized certain words of power, the kind that had been used in rituals he'd attended as a boy. Plus, his sense of hearing was fairly acute. Yet Mara acted like she was telling the truth. He let the matter go, listening as she continued to vent her emotions by relating the disturbing details of the past twelve hours.

He took exception to her suspicion of Isabel. "My grandmother would never stoop to such tactics."

Nor would he—at least, not when he was in his usual state of mind. But his relief over knowing that he wasn't involved in either the hide-doll or coyote incidents was tempered by his concern over who *was* responsible.

"Isabel told me to stay out of her dreams—"

"And what made *me* a suspect?" he cut in.

"I refused to go to bed with you."

He almost smiled. "Right. Like I can't find a willing woman when I want one."

She flushed. "Pardon my assumption. I didn't realize you were just looking for a body and a hank of hair."

The sarcasm was on target—he'd wanted Mara all right, nobody else, even as he wanted her now. This moment. Not that he would say as much.

Her cheeks remained pink as she stared at the menu. "Let's order. You promised to talk about the phone call, and I don't want to stay out all night."

Luke motioned for the waitress, who took their dinner orders and asked if they'd care for another drink.

Mara handed the woman her margarita glass. "One is enough for me or I'll be under the table."

Thinking he wouldn't mind seeing that, Luke said, "Another cola."

She rubbed her forehead. "Weirdly enough, the alcohol seems to have gotten rid of the headache I've had since last night." Her glance strayed to Luke. "Can those curse dolls cause physical pain?"

Startled, he managed to state, "I've never had any experience with them."

Though he'd heard such was possible. Not that Mara needed to know. Or that speaking a Kisi word of power was supposed to drive the pain away. He decided to put it out of his own mind before he started feeling edgy.

When the waitress returned with his cola, Mara remarked, "You don't drink?"

He took a sip. "My father was an alcoholic who died in a barroom brawl. I usually try to avoid the stuff." The beers he'd had the night before were his first in years.

"A brawl? What a tragedy. It must have been difficult for you and your mother."

Despite her annoyance with him a minute or two before, she sounded sincere. Luke had to concede that Mara was probably a nice person. Actually, more than nice. The longer he knew her, the more he realized she possessed a certain underlying serenity, a calm strength that proved she wasn't crazy. In some ways, she even reminded him of his grandmother.

Though she didn't have Isabel's training or seventy-plus wisdom. He didn't blame her for getting upset over the doll and the weird-acting coyotes.

The big yellow animal sounded like the same one that some people claimed was stalking the pueblo. Could it have been an illusion brought about by sorcery? Or had a beast been sent seventy miles south after specific prey?

He wouldn't know why a witch would hunt Mara. But then, he was confused about a lot of things lately... a white woman invading Kisi dreams, a clan elder murdered in his sleep... a fireball in the community center.

"You said you were going to talk about something unusual that happened," she said, interrupting his thoughts. "That you were going to explain your phone call."

Odd that she'd brought that up the very moment he was thinking about the disaster. Again he examined the reasons he felt compelled to confide in her. Mainly intuitive. Something invisible seemed to bind them.

"There was a fire out at the pueblo last night," he told her. "In the community center. The murals were destroyed."

"Those beautiful paintings?" Her eyes widened. "What on earth happened? Arson?"

Luke remembered the shadow in his dream, lurking just beyond his reach. "I don't think you could call sending a witchlight or a fireball arson—at least, not according to written law. And only some inner walls were burned."

"Did you see the fireball?"

"Someone told me about it."

"Then you can't be sure the fire wasn't an accident or a product of regular human malice, not something magical."

He grew impatient. "I don't have a problem accepting the supernatural. Not when it concerns Kisi magic, anyway. I've seen people call up the wind, invoke lightning." He added, "And I'm not going to spend my time trying to convince you. You have to sort out your own beliefs."

"I guess we should get back to the phone call, then. Exactly why did you want to contact me?"

"I had a nightmare."

Her blue eyes remained steady.

"A nightmare about fire," he went on. "A building was burning."

"Some sort of premonition?"

"Worse." He hesitated before sharing something he'd never revealed to anyone else. "I was asleep between three and four in the morning, which is when the fire started." He went on to explain, "I never developed my powers as a storm-bringer, never learned how to call up lightning or create fireballs." Pausing again, he decided he wasn't yet ready to admit that he feared the darkness within him, that it could be twisted and destructive. "With some people, if they find themselves in the wrong situation, if their skills are raw, they could abuse them."

She remained quiet for several seconds. "You think you caused the fire?"

"It might be possible...while I was sleeping. Maybe I created a fireball with my dream."

"You fear your subconscious that much? But this situation doesn't make sense. Why would you want to destroy your own murals?"

"Who knows? I have mixed feelings about a lot of things."

Mara continued to act pensive as the waitress arrived with their dinners. She wasn't eating much, only a bowl of chili and some tortillas.

He didn't want her to think he was asking for her sympathy. "You needled me about nightmares before, so I'm telling you. I called last night to see if you were all right, to see if you were dreaming about fire, too." More importantly, he'd wanted to reassure himself that she hadn't been *in* a fire.

"How do you know I wasn't dreaming about fire?"

"I would've been able to tell from the tone of your voice. We've shared a dream. We're connected somehow."

Might as well admit it.

She shook her head. "You're better than I am at all of this. Mysticism makes my head spin."

Obviously, she didn't know how special she was. White or not, she had power. "You have special abilities." And whether she liked it or not, just like him. "You can dreamwalk. Might as well get used to the idea."

"I can dreamwalk. Dreamwalk," she repeated, her gaze faraway. "I can go into other people's dreams."

Right. And at least she didn't have to worry about abusing her abilities. As he'd sensed from the very beginning, she had little or no darkness lurking inside her.

Having gotten a few things off his chest, he turned to his food, wolfing down his *carne asada,* a plate of steak with a side of rice and beans. In contrast, Mara merely picked at the chili and tortillas. Wondering why she wasn't hungry, he glanced up to see a big tear rolling down her cheek.

He hated it when women cried. "What's the matter with you?"

More tears filled her eyes, and she dabbed at them with her napkin. Damn it, he hoped it wasn't something he'd said.

"Maybe my fatigue is catching up with me," she murmured, "but I can't help thinking about dreamwalking, that I can actually do it." She took a shaky breath. "I didn't realize the significance, Luke. I let someone die."

He frowned. "No one's dead." Except Victor Martinez, and she hadn't even known the man.

"You don't understand. It happened before I came to Santa Fe." More tears. More dabbing as she struggled to pull herself together. "I—I had a patient ... who asked me to come into his dreams and save him from a monster. I said I couldn't..." Her voice trailed off.

"And the monster killed him?"

"A monster...something inside himself. He committed suicide soon after he got out of the hospital." Her expression was tortured. "I can dreamwalk, Luke.... I can dreamwalk like he asked me to do, but I let him die."

Now she couldn't stop the soft sobs. Her shoulders shook.

Unable to remain aloof, Luke slid an arm around her, pulling her closer, forcing himself to hold his phyical attraction at bay and tend to her immediate need. Her pain was sharp, deep, palpable enough for him to feel. He wanted to take away her pain, to take it on himself because he was used to it and she wasn't.

What was he starting up with her? With himself?

He tried to be reassuring. "You didn't know you could dreamwalk then. You can't even control it now. There was nothing you could do."

"I can't be sure."

"Yes, you can. The only reason you were able to enter my dream or my grandmother's was because we also have dreamwalking abilities."

At least, that's what he was going to insist. He stroked her hair away from her face, cradled her as closely as he could, considering their separate chairs. At the same time, he noticed an older couple staring at them from a neighboring table. To others, it probably looked like they were having a lovers' quarrel.

Lovers.

For Luke now knew that's what he and Mara could be...at the deepest level.

It was more than sexual attraction with her.

She was more than nice. More than kind. She was intelligent, complex and feisty enough to deal with the likes of him.

It was all Luke could do not to pick her up and carry her out of the place. He wanted to be alone with her. He would need more self-control when he took her home, when he would want to come upstairs and spend the night trying to protect her from both inner pain and outside threat.

They could easily become involved.

Which was exactly what he couldn't allow himself to do.

He might not have done any messing around with dolls or coyotes, but that didn't mean he couldn't be far more dangerous.

If he truly cared about Mara, he would have to keep his distance.

Mara decided that if anyone had more than one personality, it was Luke Naha.

On one hand he could be insulting, cold, even menacing.

On the other, he could be quite civil, even caring. She'd been surprised when he'd comforted her at the restaurant, had acted genuinely sympathetic.

Touched, she'd felt bereft afterward when he'd seemed to withdraw into himself. But perhaps he was still feeling exposed after admitting his fear that he'd caused a fire. No wonder he'd never wanted to talk about his nightmares. He thought he couldn't control them, and he was probably carrying a load of guilt.

Something she knew about firsthand.

So she didn't press him for conversation on the drive home, though the usual subtle tension rode between them.

He finally broke the silence himself. "You haven't seen any strangers around your neighborhood?"

"I haven't lived in this area long enough to know who's a stranger and who isn't."

"Noticed anybody following you, hanging around your building? An Indian?"

"Just you," she said lightly.

He gave her a narrow sidelong glance. "You need to keep your eyes peeled. Obviously someone doesn't like you."

"An understatement."

"It could be worse. You've gotten warnings so far, nothing real serious," he pointed out.

"If you say so." Otherwise, the coyotes would have caught her, as he'd suggested before. "What I can't figure out is why. Who would have something against me?" If it wasn't Luke himself or Isabel.

"Maybe it has something to do with your dreamwalking ability."

She was startled. "Someone else knows about it?"

"A person with power often recognizes it in someone else."

"Power?" She wanted to laugh. "So far, dreamwalking hasn't given me anything but problems."

Plus an incredibly erotic fantasy experience with Luke, one she longed to repeat in the flesh. As he pulled up in front of her building, his face brooding, she wondered if he was also thinking about that. He put the Jeep in Park but kept the motor running.

She reached for the door handle, feeling weak and wrung out.

"Just a minute."

Surely he wasn't going to suggest he walk her to the entrance. She didn't think she could deal with another one of his good-night kisses. She'd crumple and he'd have to carry her upstairs....

He stared out through the night-dark windshield. "You don't need training to use your abilities—at least, in the simplest ways. You should look around, listen hard, try to be aware of everything you can. If you feel uneasy or uptight, take it seriously."

She'd had an uneasy feeling after the doll had landed on her balcony, all right. And today she'd been spooked when she first noticed the coyotes following her. But she couldn't bring herself to mention psychic abilities.

"You're saying to pay attention to my intuition?"

"You need to watch your back."

She felt his warmth as he leaned across her to open the glove compartment. Rummaging around, he pulled out a small leather bag with a drawstring and handed it to her.

Their fingers brushed, creating electricity. But he quickly withdrew.

She smoothed the soft leather, thinking about the way his hands had felt moving over her skin. "What's this?"

"A medicine bag. Put it under your pillow before you go to sleep tonight."

"Is it supposed to protect me?"

"Can't hurt."

"What's in it? Powdered turquoise?"

"Among other things."

Fine. She slipped the bag in her purse, figuring she could use all the help she could get. Not that she wasn't too tired and strung-out to be scared.

She felt far worse about her patient, the man she might have saved, than she feared some creep who wanted to throw hide dolls or set coyotes on her.

Or create fires. She didn't want to believe Luke guilty of such an act, unconscious or not. Actually, she realized she'd never even wanted to think him capable of more than annoying behavior and a rude mouth.

He was quiet now, tapping a restless finger on the steering wheel. "You can get out of the truck. I need to be on the road."

Speaking of rude. In spite of herself, she felt his lack of warmth like a slap in the face.

"Don't you think 'good night' would be more polite?"

"I didn't go to charm school."

Swallowing her irritation, she grasped the door handle and opened it. "Sweet dreams to you, too."

Hopefully, he caught the irony.

She could feel his eyes on her as she made her way down the walk, then put her key in the building's outer door. As she went upstairs, she listened for the sound of the truck pulling out, curious when she didn't hear anything.

Half expecting and longing to see him sitting down below, she was disappointed when she went to the sliding glass doors, only to view an empty street.

Feeling nearly as empty inside, she tossed her coat on the couch and headed for the bedroom. Then, remembering the medicine bag, she returned for her purse.

Not that she intended to let anything or anyone stop her from sleeping tonight.

Even Luke. Even if he turned up on her doorstep in an uncharacteristically charming mood.

Rays of light streamed down from the opening above her. A narrow ladder stretched upward, casting shadow lines on the mud walls.

She worked the heavy stone back and forth, the earthen floor beneath her cool. Grinding corn was comforting, familiar work.

And it kept her from thinking about her dilemma....

She glanced up when she heard voices in the adjoining room. Pale moccasins appeared outside the low door, then a graying head as an elder stooped to come inside.

The woman wore the usual traditional attire—black dress with a green-and-red woven belt, a necklace of turquoise. "We know what you have been doing."

She added more kernels of corn, continued the grinding rhythm, kept her eyes respectfully lowered.

"It is not seemly," the woman went on. "And in this time, it is very dangerous. You must stop. All of us agree. You are risking the lives of your people."

Stop? To do so would be giving up her own life....

Which is what she was still thinking when she stood high above on the cliff sometime later. Dusk stole over the red land and her heart beat with anticipation.

She had seen him approaching, knew he was climbing the secret path even now. A tiny star winked far above as she moved toward an outcropping of rock, a copse of junipers.

Longing filled her, driving away most of her guilt. She nearly cried out when she heard his footfalls. But she must be quiet. She must be careful.

Finally, the lean figure of a warrior appeared. She knew those arrogant shoulders, those muscled arms, those lean hips.

"You," he said. He didn't smile, but she could feel the heat from his eyes.

His chest was bare, his hair long and loose. He wore an eagle feather, the proof of his courage.

"Come here," he ordered gruffly. "It's been too long."

"There's been danger." But she forgot about that, about hiding from enemies as he embraced her. "You need have no concern for my devotion. You fill my every thought."

"Then leave with me this day."

But torn as she was, she could not make promises. Instead, she led him past the junipers and threw a blanket onto the ground. With a growl, he lifted her dress over her shoulders and threw it aside. His eyes lit with fire at the sight of her lush body. He settled her against him, her breasts flattening against the hard wall of his chest.

She moaned as he angled his head to take her mouth. She opened her lips for him, just as she would open her body, just as she had opened her heart.

He slid hands, callused by hunting and fighting, over her smooth skin. She'd washed herself with sweet-smelling yucca—even her hair—in preparation.

He pulled her down on the blanket, loosened her leggings, cast them away with her moccasins.

Slipping a hand inside his breechcloth, she touched the strength and heat of his desire. Warmth coiled within her belly.

But he swore and tore her hand away, muttering something about a vixen. Then he cupped her breasts, teasing the sensitive tips with his fingers and his mouth. At the same time, he spread her legs to pleasure her.

She writhed, biting her lips to keep from making noise. When she couldn't stand any more, she reached for him again.

"Now," she whispered.

He'd unfastened his breechcloth and rolled over on his back. Then he lifted her above him, sliding her down his hard length.

She groaned, the earth spinning.

He arched, plunging, rocking her. She threw her head back, her spirit flying high on the wind.

She said his name, opened her eyes to see his face suffused with passion. The rugged lines were as beloved and familiar as the land that had given birth to both of them.

He lifted her hips, thrust harder and faster. Soon she was lost, climbing to the heights, shattering, drifting down again. They lay together for some time afterward, two warm bodies wrapped in a blanket.

She stroked the hard planes of his face. "Luke."

"Mara," he murmured, cradling her.

He knew her, just as she knew him.

They were together body and soul, as they'd always been meant to be, no matter who said it was wrong.

*Once again, the landscape changed...wavering like
a vision...slowly becoming the broad, barren floor of
a canyon.*

*She was hot, exhausted, thirsty. Every part of her
body hurt. Her tongue was swollen, her lips cracked.
Her feet burned.*

Her heart had left her.

*Head bowed, she could barely move her heavy legs,
even when she heard the pounding sound.*

Thud, thud, thud. Thud, thud, thud.

Something terrible was sweeping down upon her!

*She tried to run. The earth shook. Her pursuer was
relentless, drawing loud, fiery breaths. A shadow
loomed over her, cutting off the sun.*

She was going to die!

*She deserved to die, she thought, falling as slowly
as if in a dream.*

A dream?

This is a dream.

*A dream. The words sang through her mind,
whipped across the mesa with the wind, bounced off
the sides of the surrounding mountains like a trium-
phant drumbeat.*

With great difficulty, Mara Fitzgerald struggled to
her feet and finally turned to face her enemy. "This is
not over!" she screamed at him.

Not any more than it was over between her and
Luke.

CHAPTER EIGHT

Luke certainly had invaded her dreams, Mara thought, unable to get him off her mind as she finished the paperwork on Saturday.

And what a dream. A scenario realistic enough to eclipse any virtual reality game that existed. Starting with something involving Indians, the dream had progressed to an all-out, erotic love scene. Emotions—longing, passion, bittersweet sadness—had swept her away, until she was reveling in sensation, reaching an explosive physical fulfillment.

Even her decades-old chase nightmare had been affected. Mara couldn't remember exactly how the lovemaking scene had concluded, changed, how she'd ended up running across burning land yet again. But this time had been different. She'd turned and defied her pursuer. Afterward, she'd slept deeply, soundly, then had awakened filled with hope.

Though hope for what, she wasn't exactly certain.

No more than she knew whether Luke had taken part in any of this. Perhaps she'd only conjured his image, not dreamwalked. The setting hadn't been the same mesa where they'd met before. And he certainly hadn't acted interested in her last night after dinner, having left her with a medicine bag instead of a more personal gesture.

Pondering that, she stopped at a bookstore before going home. She purchased several new texts on lucid dreaming and Southwestern Indian religion, then headed back for the gallery, where she'd left her car. After the coyote incident, she'd decided it was safer to drive.

Taking a shortcut across Santa Fe's central square, she suddenly felt an odd sensation and remembered Luke's warning about trusting her instincts. Uneasy, she glanced about, sighting nothing more threatening than two tourists buying some silver jewelry from an Indian woman who had a blanket stretched across a bench. Beyond this transaction, several cars were parked on the other side of the square. One of the vehicles was a dusty black Jeep Commanche.

Luke.

Her pulse sped up.

He sat with the window down, staring. Had he been spying on her? For what reason? And if so, he obviously didn't know how or couldn't care less about keeping a low profile.

Adrenaline surging, emotions mixed, Mara approached him with determination. She might as well take the offensive. She was tired of Luke Naha sneaking up on her, playing games with her, making her feel uncomfortable. She headed for his side of the street, stopping near the Jeep. His black gaze was relentless, but she forced herself to ignore the flutters in her stomach, to smile.

"You told me to watch out for Indians hanging around. Were you referring to dreams, too?" Before he could answer, something made her add, "Was it as good for you as it was for me last night?"

A real look of surprise crossed his features. But he recovered quickly. "Yeah, it was damned good."

So they *had* shared a dream.

And she was going to blush, damn it. Warmth creeping out from her center, Mara managed to keep her own gaze steady and to steer the subject in a slightly different direction. "Do you remember the part about the other Indians? The cliff dwelling?" Images she couldn't quite focus on.

"All I remember is that I climbed some hellishly steep path. You were waiting at the top with a blanket and we—"

"Made love," she said quickly.

There'd been true feelings involved, though she certainly hoped that they were just part of the dream and not reality. What a disaster that would be.

"So what do you want now?" he asked, his strong brown hand sliding over the steering wheel. One eyebrow twitched and his voice went all low and husky. "A repeat performance?"

She should have known he'd make light of the situation. She swallowed disappointment, refusing to acknowledge it as hurt. "Don't try to cheapen things, Luke. We shared a beautiful experience." She couldn't stop herself from adding, "Probably because I thought you were someone else."

Then she turned her back and started to walk off.

The creak of the door told her he had gotten out to follow. He caught up in a couple of long strides. "What do you mean, I was someone else?"

Luke *had* been someone else, at least at first. "My dream lover wore a breechcloth and an eagle feather. He was some kind of warrior."

He caught hold of her, the warmth of his fingers sending tingles running up and down her spine. "I don't care what you thought I was wearing. You knew it was me."

"Not until the end." After she'd reached an explosive fulfillment. Just remembering made her thighs quiver. "By then it was too late."

He stared down at her. "What are you trying to do—make me jealous?"

It pleased her to knock some of the cockiness from him. "Why should you be jealous? We've never so much as been on a real date." Unless she counted the hours they shared the night before. "Or is that why you're in town again—to rectify the situation?"

She said it lightly as though she didn't care, but the truth was that she did care. After that dream, even thinking about spending another evening in Luke's company sent her senses reeling.

"You think I'm in town because I want a date?"

"What other reason could you have for being here?" Mara asked sweetly. "Something nefarious?" Then she suddenly remembered she had reason to be suspicious of him.

But he looked blank.

"Nefarious," she repeated. "It means—"

He cut in, "I know the word. I'm not stupid." He looked around. "And I'm not in town alone. I brought Rebecca and Grandmother."

"Oh." Chagrin added to disappointment, though she tried her best not to show it.

"I don't think it's such a good idea," Luke said. "Our running around together."

Now she was insulted. "Okay, I see how it is." She turned on her heel. "I'm sure I can dig up somebody else to spend time with."

He caught her arm again, but she shook him off. "You need to be careful, Mara."

"Careful. Right."

Though he himself certainly hadn't offered any more protection than a medicine bag.

Stalking back up the sidewalk, she sighted Rebecca helping Isabel into the Jeep. The woman smiled and nodded, acting as if nothing were wrong.

Perhaps nothing was. Except that Mara's world was full of sorcery, danger, dreamwalking and a man who refused to get any closer than her dreams.

Luke drove back to the reservation in a foul mood, thinking about Mara having dinner with another man. Even more obsessed with the woman after their latest dream, he'd felt heart-pounding excitement when he'd seen her walking toward him today. Not that he'd let on.

Unfortunately, the thrill had only escalated when she'd proceeded to tease him, then goad him. It had taken all his strength not to forbid her to see another man . . . and to get the hell out of there.

He could still taste her lips, savor her smooth skin. Furthermore, he could still hear the little quiver in her voice when she'd thought he was rejecting her. He'd hated himself for doing that, but had known it was necessary.

Wasn't it?

Brooding about the situation, he paid little attention to his grandmother and Rebecca until they were almost home. Then he realized the women had remained silent for quite a few miles.

He glanced at Isabel.

"We made a corn pattern yesterday," she told him, knowing, as usual, when he was looking at her. She referred to a method of reading the future and gaining insight into the present by executing a design with multicolored corn kernels. Isabel intoned, "This pattern spoke of an ancient one."

"Uh-huh," he muttered as he turned onto pueblo land and drove toward their house.

"Rebecca and I believe that we must talk to every person in the pueblo, even the smallest child. Great change is coming. And great danger."

Danger? Apprehensive, Luke thought of the shadow in his nightmare, a lurking presence he'd never experienced before.

"Charlie Mahooty won't like it if we speak to everyone in the pueblo," said Rebecca. "He thinks we're causing problems already."

"It doesn't matter," said Isabel. "We must do our duty."

Luke brought the Jeep to a halt beneath the cottonwood tree and got out to help the elder ladies. The leaves whispered in the breeze above them, casting fluttering shadows across the cool earth.

Isabel waited patiently while he unloaded some packages of yarn they'd purchased in downtown Santa Fe. "We saw a white woman in the pattern, with eyes the color of the sky."

That got his full attention. Blue eyes?

"I haven't said anything until now, Luke, but I can feel the strength of the connection between you and

Mara Fitzgerald. I could hear it in your voices when you spoke to each other."

"And I could see it in the way you two were acting together today," Rebecca added.

He didn't know whether to be spooked or annoyed. Perhaps he couldn't hide from scrutiny, but he objected, anyway. "We only shared some dreams."

"Dreams? More than one?" asked Isabel.

He couldn't lie. "Two." Two humdingers.

"A definite connection." His grandmother nodded. "And Mara has power, undeveloped though it may be. I have never before heard of such in the case of a white woman, but I believe she is also connected to the Kisi."

He knew about the power and Mara's connection with him, but he was stunned that his grandmother might think she had something to do with the entire pueblo. "You've been thinking on this?"

Isabel raised her chin, her blind eyes focused within. "I've used every skill that I have to seek true vision. I saw the serpent."

"Palolokon." Rebecca spoke the sacred name softly, with great reverence. "The spirit of wisdom."

"A blue snake." A feeling nudging him deep down, Luke recalled what he'd seen during their dreams. "Mara Fitzgerald has a tattoo of a serpent on her shoulder."

Rebecca's eyes widened.

"Does she know what the symbol means?" asked Isabel.

Thankful once again that he wasn't being asked exactly how he'd happened to see it, he said, "I don't think Mara knows what anything means." At least, not yet.

"Power that is not fully developed," said Isabel. "And possibly a sign. Perhaps *she* is an ancient one."

Suddenly appearing shocked, Rebecca protested, "You never mentioned this before. The woman isn't even an Indian."

Luke was left speechless.

"God...the saints, the spirits act in ways we do not always understand," continued Isabel. "I have come to believe that many things are possible."

"But ancestors have always been reborn as Kisi," Rebecca said, remaining upset. "We need a council of elders, many dreamseekers, to consider something so important. At the very least, we need both male and female power." She looked at Luke. "You were born to be a storm-bringer. You're young and strong. Why aren't you assuming your responsibilities?"

The accusation set his teeth on edge. He wasn't about to reveal his innermost feelings to her. "I'll take your things into the house," he told his grandmother. "Then I have to get to work on my paintings."

His refuge and salvation at the moment. Toiling like a man possessed, he'd completed one piece the night before last and was close to finishing another. Executed in acrylic, rather than oil, they'd even dry fast enough to give to the gallery.

Mara would be suprised.

Mara. If Isabel thought she might be an ancient one, her mysterious stalker might sense that, as well.

Concerned about that, he headed for the yard to collect some brushes he'd left to dry in the sun. One seemed to be missing from the weathered table on which he'd placed it, which annoyed the hell out of him. He was searching when he heard Rebecca approaching.

Her jaw was rigid and her eyes snapped. "I was serious when I reproached you about assuming your responsibilities, Luke."

He tried to hide his irritation, realizing the woman was troubled. She didn't usually act like this.

"I've never chosen to take that path. You already know that. You also know I'd need years of training." With an elder storm-bringer, a tradition that had ended with Victor Martinez.

"We don't have time but we'll have to do our best. *You* need to do your best," she admonished. "I'm setting aside some hours tomorrow. Come by my house in the morning—six a.m."

Her tone grated on him. "I don't think so."

"You *will* do this, Luke."

"Sorry, no one tells me what to do."

"I can tell you. I'm an elder."

Even his own grandmother treated him with more respect. He could feel his aggravation growing and, intent on leaving, gathered what brushes were still there.

"Don't walk away from me. How can you let Isabel assume all this pressure? If she dies an early death, it will be your fault."

He halted, guilt twisting his gut, adding fuel to his anger. "That's enough. Don't ever speak to me like this again." He glared at the woman. "I'm going to my studio before I say something we'll both be sorry for."

Even so, she prattled on as he strode away. But he wasn't listening. He swore under his breath.

If he could do something to help his grandmother, if he didn't fear he could do more harm than good, he would have taken action a long time ago.

Luke tossed and turned in bed that night, too tired to paint but unable to sleep. He imagined Mara in *her* bed, wearing some wisp of a nightgown. He'd love to be running his hands over her sweet flesh, their dream the night before having merely whetted his appetite.

She'd better not be with another man.

Once again jealous, resentful, he sat up, gazed around the night-gray room, then finally rose to head for the window. A moon shone brightly, white and full. The same light would be flooding Santa Fe, glowing down on Mara seventy miles away.

Surely she felt their connection. He tried to concentrate, send his thoughts to her.

The question was, did the connection pose a danger?

But with the mood he was in, Luke couldn't help but be reckless. His emotions and body ruled his head. If he slept tonight, would he meet her again? Would they make love yet another time?

Unfortunately, he had no answer. He could no more control his pleasant dreams than his horrific ones.

The moon resembled a huge, pockmarked, featureless face. And it seemed to be growing larger, as if it wanted to eat up the sky.

Hallucination.

He blinked and tried to get his wandering vision under control, swallowing against the bile rising in his throat. He still hadn't gotten used to the peyote. At least it was everything the Yaqui had promised it would be. He was gaining power by miles, not inches.

Though the Yaqui could offer only limited help when it came to dreams. He'd had to turn to himself, had had to practice. Tonight he wanted to use his new skills to do more than float witchlights around the pueblo or call up a few coyotes.

He settled back for the exhausting task he'd set for himself, knowing he had to conserve energy. He lay back in the darkness, concentrating, focusing his mind on the images of the place he'd memorized as sacred....

Soon he was floating above the building, rising with the wind, higher and higher until he could see the entire pueblo, a cluster of dark, dismal houses in the moon-silvered hills.

It took some time, some careful listening, to hear the dreams whispering through the night. Usually nonsense, a collection of disjointed images....

He stared down at Isabel's house as he passed over, aware that she stirred restlessly within. Uneasy, he felt anger, a thrill of fear. His unease had been growing ever since he'd realized there'd been dreamwalking the night before and that it had involved a stranger connected to Isabel, many miles away.

The white bitch. What power did she yield?

He snarled, wishing he'd killed the woman when he had the chance, not played little tricks on her.

But this was no time for fury. He forced himself to steady, to maintain control. He would leave the white woman for another time.

Better to go after the old ladies.

Isabel was going to be the more difficult, so he'd start with the other one. As he stroked the dishrag he'd stolen from Rebecca's clothesline, the token meant to help him get closer to her, he imagined his dream body floating downward, hovering over her home.

He could feel her sleeping. She wasn't dreaming yet, but he readied himself for the opening....

It came, barely minutes later. With glee, he slipped in as a shadow, then transformed himself into a sacred spirit, complete with mask, slow dancing movements and ritual weapons, including a long, sharp knife.

Rebecca was mesmerized. Her eyes were wide behind the glare of her glasses.

Then he slowly conjured up the image of the old woman's pretty granddaughter, the girl lying asleep in her dormitory. The sacred spirit danced down the hallway outside and entered the room. The girl opened her eyes in time to see moonlight shining off his blade.

No! the dream-Rebecca yelled.

He laughed, snarled, roared, jabbed, sliced... chortled as he felt the desperation of the old woman's heartbeat. She was tossing, turning, struggling as he continued his attack. Unlike Victor Martinez, she did not fear death for herself, but she was fiercely protective of her granddaughter.

She sought to manifest herself.

Go ahead. *He was ready to pounce.*

When Rebecca appeared, he came at her full force, shouting, "This is Ginnie, old woman. This is real!" Then he cut off the girl's head and dangled it above her bed by her long black hair.

He laughed as Rebecca's aging heart pounded, pounded... wavered... weakened...

Laughing in triumph, his thoughts turned to others he could affect. If nothing else, if he had the strength, perhaps he could use another stolen object to send its owner a little replay.

CHAPTER NINE

The sun had risen and birds were chirping when Luke woke.

But he hardly noticed, remaining lost to the night. Mouth dry, heart hammering, he could still envision his nightmare—a woman had died, hacked to pieces by a masked spirit wielding a long, sharp knife. And he was almost certain the victim had been an Indian.

The very idea made him sweat, for, in the second dream he'd shared with Mara, she'd been dressed as an Indian. The night before he'd been jealous, angry. And now he felt sick as he held off pure terror. What if he had entered her dream only to kill her?

Swinging his legs over the edge of the bed, Luke fought his fear, sought coherence, let his pulse decelerate . . . and slowly became aware of a wailing.

Penetrating, poignant, a voice rose and fell in a drawn-out cry of grief.

A voice that was coming from his own home.

Panicking—his first thought was that something had happened to his aged grandmother—Luke jumped to his feet and pulled on his jeans. He ran out into the hall, then through the living room, following the awful sound straight into the kitchen where Onida wrapped a blanket around his nightgown-clad grandmother, then held her.

"What the hell is wrong?"

Onida's eyes were wide and dark. Tear tracks stained her cheeks. "Rebecca is dead."

"Rebecca?" Not Mara. He hadn't expected this, felt dazed, confused. "How—?"

"*He* killed her, Luke." Isabel spoke so fervently, her fragile body shook. "In the night, he came into her dreams and took her."

"Who?"

"The evil one, the person who is stalking this pueblo. I woke thinking I'd felt his presence this morning. I ran to Rebecca's side for help. But he'd been there before me. She was drawing her last breath."

Horrified, mind spinning, Luke saw Rebecca in his mind's eye, heard their argument the day before. He'd been angry with her as well as with Mara....

Had *Rebecca* been the victim in his dream?

"How could anyone kill an elder?" Onida asked.

"By being clever enough to frighten the life from her." Isabel shivered, clutching at the blanket. "She was old and had no one to protect her." Her face twisted in grief. "I should have known better. I should have realized he was growing stronger. I should have never let Rebecca leave my presence—together we could have fought him."

Her regret pierced Luke to the heart, while his own sorrow twisted his guts. He'd cared about Rebecca, had grown up with her. She'd been like an aunt. She'd tried demanding his help and he'd turned on her. Now she was dead.

And it was his fault.

Onida helped the elderly woman to the table. "Sit down. I'll make you some toast and warm milk."

"I cannot eat or drink."

"You have to eat and drink, Grandmother," Luke insisted. "You can't afford not to."

"He will take me next. What use is there?"

He'd never heard her say such things before. He met his mother's worried glance.

"No one's going to take you," he swore fiercely. "I'll kill them if they try."

Including his damned self, should he have been the one....

Though surely he wouldn't harm his own grandmother. But if he found out he had the slightest murderous inclination, had been in the least way responsible for this tragedy, he would take a one-way trip straight off a high cliff before he could hurt anyone else.

"She said, 'Ginnie,'" Isabel murmured. "That's all. I don't know what it means."

Ginnie? Rebecca's granddaughter, the girl who was going to college.

The name brought forth a host of images. In his dream, an Indian woman had been killed...young, with long black hair and a pretty, innocent face. Startled, Luke suddenly knew he'd seen Ginnie die. The setting of the nightmare had been proof of that, as well. Luke could still see the blood-spattered walls of the dormitory room, the girl's head hanging by its hair and dripping onto the bed sheets....

He grimaced, feeling sick.

"Luke?" His grandmother obviously sensed his confusion, his agony.

He reached for her hand and held it too tightly. "I said I will take care of you."

"I know your intentions are good."

Were they? Or was she blind on more than one level, unable to sense the sins of her own blood? Luke only wished he knew for certain that he was guilty. But if he wasn't, how had he come to know so many details?

Onida placed a plate of toast and a cup of warm milk in front of Isabel. "Come now. Eat." She also told Luke. "You sit down, too. I'll take care of phoning the rest of Rebecca's relatives." All of whom lived off the reservation. "I already talked to Ginnie and her parents."

He seized on the name. "Ginnie?" She was alive.

"I felt she should know as soon as possible." Again, his mother gestured for him to be seated and he sank numbly into a chair.

Where he took a deep breath. Ginnie was alive. At least he should be happy for that.

But the relief was only temporary.

Just as he'd known it had been Ginnie in his nightmare, he now knew what had killed Rebecca. She'd said Ginnie's name before dying. She'd experienced the same macabre vision he'd glimpsed in his nightmare. A vivid illusion meant to frighten her to death.

But whose illusion? His own? Or someone else's? A shadow had stalked him through the dream of fire. Someone had tried to terrorize Mara with a curse doll and marauding coyotes.

Mara. God help him, even in this hellish crisis, Luke wanted to reach out to her.

If nothing else, he needed to make absolutely certain she was all right... and to make sure she stayed that way.

* * *

Mara woke up clearheaded but very depressed. Something seemed terribly wrong.

After reading for several hours the night before, she'd fallen into a peaceful, uninterrupted sleep.

So what was the matter?

Shadows seemed to be creeping about the borders of her consciousness. Once again, she remembered Luke telling her to trust her instincts. Because of that, when the phone shrilled beside her bed, she sprang straight up. Clutching the sheet, her hand unsteady, she reached for the receiver, dragging it to her ear. "Hello?"

"Mara?"

"Luke?" Now what? Tension crackled through the phone. "Don't hang up on me. Not again."

"I'm not going to hang up. But I can't talk long—I'm on the pay phone near the pueblo store. Things have taken a turn for the worse. I just wanted to tell you to be even more careful."

"What has gotten worse?" She felt a surge of anxiety. "You're not telling me everything. You haven't from the beginning—"

He cut in, "Rebecca's dead."

Her stomach knotted.

Rebecca. The nice lady who'd crocheted and who'd been so proud of the granddaughter who was going to graduate from college.

Mara couldn't believe it. "How? Where?"

"She passed away in bed."

"Was she sick?"

He hesitated, then said, "The report will probably chalk it up as a heart attack."

"Meaning you don't think it was?"

"That isn't your problem. I'm simply telling you to watch yourself."

Why? Because he cared so much? Warmth crept through her. And again she thought about what had passed between them in their shared dream. About the real feelings that rose beyond lust.

"What more can I do to take care of myself?" she asked. "Bathe myself in turquoise powder? Buy an automatic weapon? And I *do* think Rebecca's death is my problem. Since I found out about dreamwalking, I've realized I'm involved with all of you." Suddenly she also knew why he sounded so uptight. "You think someone killed Rebecca, don't you? Did she have medication that could have been tampered with—?"

"Whatever killed her came from inside."

Deep down, something within her wasn't surprised. She swallowed. "You're not talking about a dream, surely?"

His silence told her that he was.

"Someone entered her dream? This witch person, the same one who was warning me?"

"Possibly. No one knows, including Grandmother."

That Luke seemed unsure bothered her. That Isabel felt confused frightened her more than she could say.

"I've never seen my grandmother this upset in my life," Luke went on.

An honest, anxious statement that exposed uncharacteristic vulnerability.

"Isabel is the only wisewoman left," Mara murmured. No wonder Luke was troubled enough to let his guard down. "Does she feel she's in danger, too?"

Again, Luke was silent, scaring Mara all the more. A nightmare monster was stalking Isabel? Horror stabbed at her like a knife.

She fought it with stubborn resolve. "I'm coming out there."

"No one's inviting you."

"I don't care. And don't waste your time trying to make me feel unwelcome or uncomfortable. You said I should listen to my inner feelings and they're screaming for me to go." She was compelled to be by his side. "I'll see you in a couple of hours."

He didn't object again, she noticed, as she hung up. Then she was out of bed, flying to the shower, to the closet, scrambling out the door.

She drove over the speed limit all the way to the Kisi pueblo.

When she pulled through the gate, a stream of sober-faced folk, some carrying dishes of food, were heading toward a little house up the hill from Luke's. At least half a dozen vehicles were parked in the driveway. Assuming the place must be Rebecca's, Mara pulled her own car over to the side of the road and approached.

The nearest door stood open, revealing knots of people standing around in the kitchen. Mara slipped inside, trying to ignore the way everyone suddenly stopped talking and stared.

"I was a friend of Rebecca's," she announced.

For whatever reason, the crowd parted before her. Beyond the kitchen, in the living room, more people had gathered. Many were talking to Isabel, who sat beside Onida on the blanket-covered couch. Both women wore stoic expressions but were obviously grieving. Isabel was so pale and drawn and tired looking, her bones seemed visible through her parchment skin. Mara felt worried as she observed the last wisewoman of the Kisi. If someone had been able to kill Rebecca, Isabel was also vulnerable.

Thinking about what to say, she felt a hand on her arm. A large, warm hand with strong fingers. "Luke." He stood so near, her body betrayed her. Her belly filled with heat, her breath caught in her throat.

"You can do nothing."

She frowned. "Maybe, maybe not. I've been thinking a lot over the past two hours." About issues she'd never considered before, hadn't allowed herself to believe. An adulthood of psychological, science-based reality had fallen by the wayside. "We can't allow this kind of thing to continue."

The way he looked at her told her she'd surprised him. *"We?"*

"If I actually have abilities, I'm going to develop them. I'm sure you and Isabel can help me."

His scowling brows met in a straight line. "I can't help anybody. And Grandmother is weak and tired."

"She'll soon be dead, if we don't do something. Would you rather have that?" Emotional, she couldn't stop tears from stinging her eyes. "I can't stand by and let someone die, Luke...not a second time."

"This isn't your problem."

"Quit saying that." She snuffled, wiped her nose with a tissue. She couldn't believe he was still arguing. "It's been my problem ever since I found myself in Isabel's dreaming place. If you'd use your logic, try to make sense, you would know that's true. I can dreamwalk—"

"Be quiet." His hand on her arm tightened painfully.

Angry, hurting, she started to object, then realized that the conversations around them had quieted. People were listening. She noticed Charlie Mahooty standing some feet away with his stoop-shouldered pal, Delgado. As usual, Mahooty looked far from friendly.

She smiled wanly, anyway, and placed her hand on Luke's to get him to loosen his hold. He did so as a pretty young woman with long black hair approached.

"I'm Rebecca's granddaughter, Ginnie," she said, addressing Mara. Her eyes were red, but she seemed in charge of herself. "You said you're a friend of my grandmother's?"

Mara nodded. "I'm so sorry for your loss." She meant that with all her heart. "I only met Rebecca a short time ago, but I really liked her."

Luke added, "My grandmother introduced them. Mara runs the art gallery that shows my paintings in Santa Fe."

Ginnie nodded. "It was nice of you to come. The funeral will be held day after tomorrow."

"I'll be there," Mara told her, thinking she'd once again have to juggle hours at the gallery.

But then, she'd be taking off whatever time she needed to deal with the dreamwalking. Nothing was as important as life and death.

Ginnie introduced her parents, along with a couple of other relatives who lived in the area, if not on the reservation. Mara chatted a few minutes and offered more condolences, happy that Luke stuck by her side.

As soon as Ginnie moved away, Mara headed for the couch and Isabel, with Luke in her wake. She nodded to Tom Chalas.

The man greeted her in return. He looked drawn himself, as if he was deeply affected. "You seem to be out here a lot." His tone was neutral, not unfriendly.

"I wish my visit were for a better reason today."

"Don't we all."

So Chalas was upset, too. Ginnie had said he'd donated several cases of soft drinks for this occasion. Perhaps he'd especially liked Rebecca. Thinking how decent the man seemed, how upset he'd been when she'd rejected his art some days before, she felt bad all over again.

A priest had arrived at the gathering and was drawing a chair up beside Isabel, making Mara pause. She glanced at Luke.

"He does mass here on Sunday," he said in explanation.

They both hovered some distance away as Isabel and the priest discussed Rebecca's funeral.

"I will take care of the prayer feathers she will hold," said Isabel. "And her wedding robe is in the chest at the foot of her bed."

It was the traditional burial garb for women of Pueblo descent, Mara knew from reading books about Southwestern people.

"Grandmother will guide us in special ceremonies after the priest is through," Luke told her in a low tone. "The pallbearers will be purified with juniper smoke and sacred cornmeal will be scattered from the cemetery to Rebecca's house."

So that the dead woman's soul could visit home one last time before going to the next world, Mara thought.

"She was your best friend," the priest was saying, patting Isabel's hand. He was a Hispanic man with large, sad eyes and a comforting manner. "May God give you strength."

"She was more than a friend, Padre. She was like a sister." Isabel sighed. "And she had been my eyes since I became blind."

The priest shook his head in sympathy. "A second death in so short a time. And another heart attack. But I guess many of the reservation's population are growing older."

Mara glanced at Luke. A *second* death?

He narrowed his eyes and mouthed the word *later*.

"Rebecca wasn't that old," objected Onida. "She was only sixty-six and hadn't had so much as the flu for more than a year."

"Are you saying you think there should be an autopsy?" asked the priest.

"No autopsy," Isabel said. "I have spoken with the family and no one thinks it necessary."

The priest patted Isabel's hand one last time before rising. "I need to talk to the family again myself. They say other relatives will be arriving from out of state."

Mara waited until the clergyman disappeared into the crowd. The room was buzzing with conversation again, leaving Isabel and Onida alone on the couch.

Mara took the vacated chair and leaned in close, keeping her voice low. "Isabel? I know this sounds strange, but I've come out here to try to help." Even though the woman had virtually told her to stay away from the pueblo.

Isabel turned her face in Mara's direction, recognition in her expression. She sat up straighter, looked a little stronger. She even appeared less pale and tired.

"At last. So the spirits have not abandoned us."

Spirits? Feeling nervous, hesitant, Mara pointed out, "It's just that you don't seem to have anyone else—"

"There is no need for explanation," Isabel cut in. "I will train you, Mara Fitzgerald."

Mara was surprised that Isabel reacted so positively and so swiftly. She also felt a strange underlying sense of excitement. And Luke's disapproval was evident by his hand clamping down tight on her shoulder.

"I don't know who you really are," Isabel went on, "but you are right. You—and my grandson—are my only hope in this darkness. When can you begin?" she asked.

"She can't do this," Luke growled. "It's too dangerous."

Mara ignored him. "Today? Tomorrow? How much time will it take?"

"As much as you can spare. Though I don't think you could stand more than three or four hours to start," Isabel added. "Come to my house at dawn tomorrow. I'm feeling far too weak to do anything this day."

Dawn. Calculating quickly, Mara realized she could work her gallery hours around that. This was a life-and-death matter but the material world wouldn't disappear entirely.

"What about you, Luke?" Isabel asked.

"What about me?"

"The Kisi need you, Luke. *I* need you."

"You don't know what you ask, Grandmother."

Isabel raised a brow.

"There are things you don't know, maybe because I'm your own blood," Luke insisted, sounding urgent. "I would die for you, if I had to... and maybe I should. Taking a leap off a cliff might be the best plan of action."

Then, face stormy, he turned and pushed his way through the crowd.

Mara sat there flabbergasted. Was he actually threatening to kill himself? She gazed at Onida and Isabel, assuming the poor women must be upset.

Onida's eyes were round with shock, but Isabel seemed unusually calm.

"Go talk to him," the wisewoman told Mara. "You are connected. If anyone can reach him, it is you."

Without questioning what Isabel knew about the bond with Luke or how she came to know it, Mara rose to wend her way through the growing crowd. Not an easy task—the small house was packed. Even more people were arriving as she left the front door and walked out to the road.

Luke was nowhere in sight. Wondering where he'd disappeared to so fast, she headed for his house at the bottom of the slope. She knocked on the door and, receiving no response, went on in.

"Luke?"

No answer. Feeling a bit like an intruder, Mara explored, peeking into every room. She even entered what must be Luke's private quarters, noting several paintings sitting around in the studio part, the rumpled sheets in his bedroom.

Remembering once again the passion they'd shared the night before, she stared at the bed. There was no use lying about her attraction for Lucas Naha or the bond that burned between them. If she didn't watch out, she'd be falling in love with the man.

If she wasn't already head over heels.

Concerned for his life at the moment, Mara abandoned the house when she realized it was empty. Outside, the Jeep sat quietly under the cottonwoods. So he hadn't taken a drive. Walking out to the road again, she looked all around, finally spotting a young boy petting an Appaloosa in the fenced pasture area bordering Luke's house.

She strode toward him. "Excuse me, have you seen Luke Naha?"

The boy pointed north. "He went that way."

A narrow, winding path led toward a big flat-topped, terra-cotta mesa. Beyond that lay foothills, mountains, any of which offered sheer drops.

Mara took off. She forged on until the path ended near the mesa, glad she'd worn practical pants and walking shoes. The ground was rutted, rough and sometimes torn up by hoofprints.

"Luke!"

But her voice only echoed back at her, bouncing off the sides of the mesa. She glanced up, noticing the size and shape of the flat rocky outcropping, its red color.

Lightning Over Red Mesa—this spot must have been the inspiration for Luke's painting. Not to mention that it was the setting for a dream she'd shared with Isabel and another with Luke.

But Luke wasn't here now.

Calling his name a couple more times and hearing no response, she skirted the edge of the mesa and plunged onward. The ground began to rise and footing became rougher. Rocks rolled beneath her feet and prickly desert grasses plucked at her as she passed. Soon she seemed to be isolated in nature, the mountainous horizon endless, the sky a huge blue expanse.

"Luke!"

No answer, though the sun dimmed for a moment and she glanced up to see a cloud passing over. A spray of brilliant light suddenly shot through, giving the illusion of linking sky to land. A vast, wild land that seemed very familiar.

Sun Dog. A thrill passed through her as she recognized another setting that could have inspired a Naha painting.

And she herself was the tiny figure moving around in the landscape.

The thrill turned to chills. Mara stopped dead. What was going on? Were his paintings alive? Did they shift, waver, fluctuate, change like dreams? Like life itself?

For a moment, everything seemed to flow together, human and sky and earth. She felt like she was one part of a much larger plan, an overwhelming and grandiose design.

The wind touched her cheek, but time stood still.

Time.

Minutes and days and years swirled together, with Mara standing in the middle....

She could almost see it...the cliff from which she'd gazed in her dream. There were other people, though she could feel them, not see them. There were a myriad of emotions—pain and fear, hope and resignation, love. Mara closed her eyes, taking a deep breath of the past and the present, almost able to feel the future aproaching....

Thud, thud, thud. Thud, thud, thud.

Vibrating earth. Heavy breathing. Something was coming, something large enough to cast a shadow.

Were nightmares about to blend with reality?

Mara cried out as she turned to see who or what was swooping down on her.

CHAPTER TEN

Luke locked on to Mara's shocked, frightened expression as he galloped his horse toward her. She shouted at him in Kisi. And as he reined in his lathered buckskin, she backed away, stumbling.

He dismounted, let the reins drop, went to her. "What do you think you're doing?" he growled, even as he was torn between wanting to take her in his arms and wanting to shake some sense into her. He did neither. "You shouldn't be out in the desert alone on foot. If coyotes are going to track you in Santa Fe, you could meet up with a lot worse out here."

The fearful look faded, changed to anger. He wanted to touch her in the worst way, but he could tell she wasn't exactly in a receptive mood.

"Don't you yell at me, Luke. I was searching for you. I thought you were going to throw yourself off a cliff."

As if she could stop him. Actually, he hadn't been looking for that cliff...yet. Instead, he'd saddled one of the horses he kept in the pueblo's community pasture and had ridden hell-bent for leather into the hills looking for some sort of refuge in nature.

He told her, "I wanted to get away from people."

"Like your mother and your grandmother? Don't you care that they're upset?"

"They might be better off without me."

"That's ridiculous. Because you're afraid you caused a fire?"

"More than that. I may be a murderer."

He saw questions fill her eyes. Questions that alarmed her.

"Let's take a walk," he suggested. "The horse needs to cool off." He picked up the reins and they started off.

"What made you say such a fool thing, anyway?" Mara demanded. "What kinds of things don't the rest of us know?"

"My dream this morning, for one."

Luke gave her an edited version of the illusion that had caused Rebecca's heart to stop. He could tell that the gorier details sickened her.

"How would I know such things, if I didn't create them myself?" he asked.

"But *why* would you create them? You had no reason to want Rebecca dead."

"I liked her...but I was furious with her yesterday. She tried to force me into agreeing to be trained for dreamwalking."

"You were furious enough to kill? Even someone you cared about?"

"It wouldn't be the first time," he stated flatly.

That got her attention. Her eyes widened to a startled blue. That he wanted to lose himself in those eyes, in that soft body of hers, despite the horrific situation he was trying to deal with, infuriated him. When had he lost control of his conscious self?

"I told you I can't control my powers," he said angrily. "I never could. In Arizona—"

He fell silent, thinking he'd never talked about his other life to anyone but his grandmother and mother before. He wouldn't be talking about it now if he wasn't in such a terrible situation.

"What about Arizona?" she probed as they continued to walk together.

"I lost my wife and my three-year-old son."

"They died?"

"Six years ago, in a fire."

The admission was difficult to make. It still hurt him to talk about the incident. And maybe he was a fool to do so, but he couldn't help himself. He and Mara were connected in a way that most people *couldn't* even dream about. She had a right to know the truth. Then maybe she'd be smart enough to run in the other direction, to stay far away from him.

"I'd had a fight with my wife. She was Navajo and we had a lot of problems with her family...not to mention with my temper. But she never talked about divorce before." And he'd never before felt so willing to reveal the memory. "I walked out crazy mad, got into our old pickup and took off. I don't remember where I drove or how fast. When I ran out of gas, it was dark, so I stopped and fell asleep. I had terrible dreams. The next morning, when I came home, I found the house had burned down during the night."

This time, Mara didn't hurry to his defense. Looking thoughtful, she ambled along beside him. Until the buckskin snorted. She glanced at the animal warily, seeming uncomfortable. Perhaps, having lived in San Francisco most of her life, she wasn't used to horses.

"You dreamed of fire that night in Arizona?" she asked.

"That's the theme of most of my nightmares."

"What about before you were married?"

Surprised that she wasn't probing about the deaths, he said, "Did I dream of fire? As a kid, sure."

"Did anything burn up then . . . in reality?"

"No." And that was strange, now that he thought about it.

"Did you always have a bad temper?"

"It's gotten worse over the years. And lately, well, whenever I feel angry with someone . . . I'm not sure what I'll do."

"But it sounds like you've always been temperamental. And that you've always been haunted by inexplicable nightmares, just as I have."

"The difference being that your dreams are chases, with you playing the role of the victim," he said darkly. "Mine are about fire . . . and my wife and child were victims for real."

"How can you be certain you were at fault? Wasn't there an investigation?"

"Of course. Though the fire department was baffled. They finally said that rags soaked with turpentine must have been to blame, materials I'd been using for the paintings I was working on when I wasn't out driving a truck to support my family. But the blaze was so hot, so intense, it was next to impossible to pinpoint exactly how it began."

She nodded. "Still, you might only be torturing yourself with guilt, trying to make yourself responsible . . . a classic way of dealing with grief and situations you can't control. There was no real proof that you caused the fire."

"I don't know why you're trying to offer excuses for me," he said bitterly. "Nothing will bring back two lives."

"But surely you know you have to come to terms with the tragedy. And rags could indeed have been to blame."

He couldn't let himself off the hook so easily. "I already told you I have no problems believing in the supernatural. I knew in my heart what had gone on. I dreamed of a red-hot blaze." He went on. "After everything was over, I took off, got drunk and stayed that way for months. When I finally came to my senses, I was in a small town outside of Tucson. I got a job as a dishwasher and went back to painting—art was the only thing that straightened out my brain."

They headed for flatter land, a dry riverbed. Their feet kicked up sandy earth. But there was moisture left beneath the soil, enough to allow for a few small box elders, some buckthorn and sagebrush. Beyond and around them on the rolling hills, piñons dotted the sandy earth, turning and twisting their reddish trunks as they reached for the sky.

Mara mused, "How strange. Everything that's happened seems like pieces of a puzzle, and that if only we could figure out how to put them together we could get to the truth. I was thinking about that before you rode up."

"The truth." He snorted. "Might as well chase a shadow."

He loved the way the wind was ruffling her light brown hair. Despite the seriousness of their discussion, he wanted to run his fingers through it...wanted the comfort of touching a caring human being.

Mara said, "I still don't think that you should believe you killed your wife and son. Not any more than you should presume you caused the fire in the community center...or created the horrible dream that killed Rebecca. Wouldn't that illusion be a little out of the ordinary for you, anyway? It had nothing to do with fire."

"I've occasionally had other types of nightmares. Sometimes I even walk or drive in my sleep. I don't know what I'm capable of. And I'm not exactly a nice person," he added.

She didn't disagree, but said, "That doesn't make you a murderer."

"Sounds like you don't want me to be."

Because she cared for him? But he supposed he shouldn't be considering the possibility in this dismal situation.

They'd reached the end of the flat ground and faced a jumble of boulders where the riverbed rose into the hills. They stopped, turned and went back the same way they'd come. The Kisi pueblo was visible in the distance, beyond Red Mesa. Luke spotted the dust of another vehicle entering the gates—probably more of Rebecca's relatives. He realized once again that the woman was gone, that she'd never be coming back, and his heart felt heavy as a stone.

"Why would I know all the details about the murder dream, if I wasn't the one who killed Rebecca?" he asked again, looking for more concrete reassurances.

"That I don't know," she said, "but there are quite a few unusual things going on, aren't there? Scary things. Who threw that curse doll onto my balcony and who set the coyotes on me? And didn't your grandmother say that illusions can be created in dreams, as well as in real life? Maybe that same person sent that nightmare to Rebecca, and you somehow managed to tap into it."

The possibility almost made Luke feel better. "He'd have to be pretty powerful."

"But you're not denying it could have happened. What if this person made sure you tuned into Rebecca's dream so you would think it was your fault?"

"Why would he pick on me?"

"Because you have special abilities. Power. The same reason you suggested he singled me out."

"Power." He smiled blackly. "I don't even want it."

"But we've got it. And we have to use it for good, Luke." Her tone grew in urgency. "We have to do whatever it takes to save your grandmother. She's next. Some horrible person is running amock, throwing things out of sync. He obviously wants to destroy the traditions of the Kisi. And who knows where he'll go from there."

Her tone was so empassioned, she expressed such courage, that she touched Luke more than he could say. And, God help him, he wanted her even more than he'd ever desired her before. He was aware of every nuance as she moved along beside him, the purposeful way she walked, the determined set of her chin. And because of her, he found himself mulling over the possibility of trying to harness his damnable abilities.

"This could be very, very dangerous," he growled.

For, if he were the guilty one...may God protect all those close to him.

"I don't care if it's dangerous," she was saying. "And neither should you. Wouldn't you rather die trying to help someone else than running away? You're a warrior in your heart, Luke. I can tell."

Deep down, something inside him answered to the title, told him not to be afraid of his own dark side any longer.

"We'd also better be damned good sorcerers if we're going to deal with this sicko," he said. "This isn't the first time he's killed, you know."

Her eyes widened. "Someone died before Rebecca?"

"I wasn't aware of it to begin with. The last storm-bringer priest died in his sleep a few weeks ago."

"Victor Martinez."

Luke gazed at Mara appreciatively. "You are a fast study."

"I have a good memory. Your mother mentioned that a death had upset the pueblo."

The midday sun beat down on them. Even in the high desert, noon could be very warm.

When Mara stopped to rest, leaning against a pine tree, Luke suggested they ride the rest of the way.

"The horse is cooled down now. And he might as well earn his hay."

She stared at the animal warily, thinking the buckskin seemed very tall. As well as scary somehow. "I never learned how to ride."

"No problem. You can sit behind me."

Without waiting for her agreement, he placed a foot in the stirrup and mounted with one graceful movement, then held out his hand for her.

She still balked.

"Come on." He kicked his boot free. "Put your foot right there and I'll pull you up." Then he grinned crookedly. "Where's all this courage you've been talking about?"

That did it. Mara tightened her jaw and approached the horse, lifted her foot and took Luke's hand. He easily pulled her up and, with only a little awkwardness, helped her plop down behind him in the saddle. The buckskin stirred, shifting from leg to leg. It was odd being on top of such a large, living creature.

"You're not going to go fast, are you?" she asked, trying to keep her voice cool.

"Not with the horse."

Meaning he had other plans for her?

She couldn't help thinking about the way his hands had felt on her, both in reality and dreams. She had to slide her arms about him now, in order to keep her balance. His broad back was warm, his chest hard. His muscular thighs tightened around the horse, making her wonder what they would be like naked in real life, his flesh against hers.

She sucked in a nervous breath and tried to distract herself. "Are there other strange things that have gone on out here at the pueblo?" she asked. "Besides the fire in the community center and the two elders' deaths?"

"Some people claim to have seen witchlights—glowing balls floating around some nights. Then there's this coyote that killed several sheep."

She remembered the carcass she'd seen the first day. Sights like that always seemed to haunt her. "A big yellow coyote?"

"Supposedly. With glowing red eyes."

"And people believe this animal's *controlled* by someone? Sounds like the coyote that tried to attack me in Santa Fe. But he would have had to travel a long way."

"Sorcery is sometimes real, sometimes illusion. You never know. That's what makes it doubly dangerous."

A thrill shot through her, though she wasn't certain if the disturbing sensation came more from pure apprehension or Luke's disconcerting nearness.

"I suppose you don't know what my training is going to be about?"

"You suppose right. All I ever learned was the rudiments of dreamseeking."

As the horse descended a hill, he stumbled, making Mara grasp Luke more tightly. Ignoring the taut tension between them was becoming more and more difficult.

She tried, anyway. "I'm sure I'll have to pick out a dreaming place. Learn some Kisi."

"If you don't already know it. Maybe Grandmother will just have to nudge your memories."

That remark caught her attention. "My memories? What are you talking about?"

"I've heard you speak the language more than once, in reality and dreams. Today, you said 'Who comes?' when I rode up."

"But how—?"

"The Kisi believe people are sometimes reborn."

"Reincarnation?" The idea took her breath away. She thought of her experience less than an hour ago, when time seemed to stand still. She'd been feeling a sense of cognition since first setting foot on Kisi land. "You're suggesting I was once an Indian?"

"You've also got that little tattoo on your shoulder. A blue snake is a symbol of Palolokon, the sacred serpent." He hesitated only a second before adding, "Grandmother believes you might be an ancient one, though she's never known of anyone being reborn as white."

Mara was speechless. She couldn't tell what Luke believed. "What do you think?"

"I don't think about it at all. I don't know."

Mara wasn't certain he was being truthful. "But I could have also learned this stuff some other way, right? If I have the psychic power to dreamwalk, I might also be able to pick up on a language."

"Could be," he said, remaining noncommittal.

They were passing Red Mesa, the buckskin's nose pointed toward his pasture. The horse lengthened his stride. Luke tightened the reins, probably stopping the animal from trotting. Mara knew she'd fall off if that happened.

But they arrived at the pasture gate safe and sound. Luke let her down the same way she'd gotten on, then dismounted himself.

"So you're going to agree to the training?" she asked, hoping she'd talked him into it.

"I'll try... for my grandmother."

What about for *her?* Mara felt a little twinge of jealousy, then told herself not to be petty.

"What are you thinking about?" he asked, gazing at her assessingly.

"Everything—dreams, visions." And him, of course.

"We had a real nice one last time, didn't we?"

More than nice. Intoxicating, erotic. The memory nearly took her breath away.

But she pulled herself together and said, "I think we're going to have to be serious from now on."

He stepped closer. "I was serious. I still want you."

She felt the heat from his body as he stood before her, and she automatically raised her lips for his kiss. Though she didn't expect him to embrace her quite so suddenly, to pull her so tightly against his hard body.

"Do you want me?" he asked, his mouth near hers.

"Yes. But—"

He hushed her protest with a long, harsh kiss. She closed her eyes, savoring his taste, his scent...his power. His tongue invaded and stroked the inside of her mouth. One hand at the small of her back, he slid the other up to cup her breast. It seemed to swell into his palm, the nipple hardening with desire.

But Luke demanded further intimacies, pulled her blouse free of her waistband and slipped his hand beneath it. He left a trail of gooseflesh as he slipped his hand upward. Her lacy bra posed no barrier to him. Mara moaned softly as he sought her breast again, caressed her naked flesh.

In turn, she touched him, sliding her hands along the shirt stretched over his chest. Heat surged through the material to sear her palms.

Her knees felt weak as he broke their kiss and nuzzled her neck. Then he moved lower...

And Mara suddenly realized that if she didn't put a stop to this fevered exploration, they would make love...in broad daylight, in public. She knew the pasture was visible from several buildings, including Rebecca's house and the burned-out community center.

"Luke." She didn't want to push him away emotionally, but physically she had no choice. She struggled for breathing room. "Someone could be watching."

"I don't care."

But she did. And she couldn't help longing for a time when she could trust Luke... at least trust his feelings. She couldn't help wishing he'd choose a word other than *want* when expressing his desire for her. Even *connection* or *bond* would do. Luke had admitted he'd felt a bond in their dreams.

He seemed to notice that she'd stiffened and wasn't responding. He loosened his hold, raised his head and looked at her.

"Now what's the matter?" he demanded, an irritating impatience creeping into his voice. "You would have been ready for this yesterday."

"But yesterday you weren't interested." She emphasized the reminder by pushing at his chest. "Not to mention that you left me at my doorway the night before without so much as a good-night kiss. That's a big part of the problem between us, Luke. You blow hot and cold." She turned his words back on him. "What's the matter with *you?*"

His mouth formed a straight line and he released her completely. "I've been telling you what's wrong with me. Not that you seem to believe it."

He was back to his old angry self.

Sorrow sluiced through her. "Looks like we get along better in our dreams."

"Even if it's sacrilege, hmm?"

"Sacrilege? What do you mean?"

"I was always told dreamwalking should be used for healing and wisdom," he told her. "It's not meant for playing around with sex."

Sacrilege, indeed, because he was calling what they had shared "sex" rather than "making love," Mara realized.

Angry herself, feeling cheated by his seemingly un-
caring attitude, she turned her back on him and strode
away. "I'm going back to talk to your grandmother,
then head for Santa Fe before it gets dark."

Luke made no reply at all and he didn't try to stop
her. When she glanced over her shoulder, he had his
back turned as he unsaddled the horse.

Damn him.

But she needed to remember that the task before
her—before *them,* unless Luke backed out—was the
most important task she'd ever chosen to undertake.

The road stretching south to Santa Fe appeared
empty of other vehicles. Mara felt isolated and alone.

Rebecca was dead. Isabel was being threatened.
And Luke seemed to think he was a demon incarnate.

He'd been convincing enough to sow some doubts.
Remembering the horrific dream-illusion he'd described—Ginnie's head hanging by its hair—Mara
couldn't help recalling the time he'd come to her rescue in the community center and threatened to tear off
Charlie Mahooty's head.

Had a lifetime of nightmares twisted him, filled him
with such anger? What truly fueled his fiery intensity?

And why did she care so much, anyway?

Perhaps the feelings, the emotional longings. Luke
had aroused in her during their shared dreams had
been illusions, as well. Lies.

She sighed, then tried to push the negative thoughts
from her mind. Isabel had told her to try to keep her
mind clear and serene. She'd also suggested Mara not
eat anything before coming to the pueblo the next day.

While thinking on that, she spotted a tan body hurtling down a hill near the road. The pronghorn antelope took a great leap, its rump flashing white.

Wondering why the animal, a herd beast, seemed to be on its own, Mara noticed a tight curve ahead just in time to check her speed. A two-foot metal barrier stood between the car and a steep drop.

Eyes steady, both hands on the steering wheel, she didn't expect to see the pronghorn suddenly come out of nowhere to leap the barrier and bound across the road directly in front of her.

Instinctively reacting, she slammed the brakes so hard the car fishtailed with a squeal of rubber. But there was no collision. She'd avoided hitting the animal, thank God. Her heart pounded as she brought the vehicle to a shuddering, complete stop. Breath shaky, she sat there for a moment, car nearly sideways in the road, thinking all she needed was an accident with a hundred-pound-plus creature.

She couldn't remain parked in the middle of the road. Nosing the car back into the right lane, she took off, slowly picking up speed again. The state of New Mexico wasn't kidding with all the warning signs of deer crossings.

The road wound up the side of one rugged mountain, then descended, only to climb yet another. Shaky though she was, she didn't allow her mind to wander, not even for a few seconds. The country was rough between the Kisi reservation and Santa Fe. Miles passed and more barriers lined the curves, several dented in places from run-ins with straying vehicles.

Mara found herself eyeing the road's shoulder, as well as the dense brush that grew on the opposite side.

Still, when another pronghorn emerged from a copse of junipers, this one running diagonally toward her, she was startled.

Heart in her throat, she knew she couldn't avoid the animal but tried desperately, anyway. The car swerved, fishtailed again, this time the rear crashing into the barrier. Metal squealed across metal in a spray of sparks. Something clunked, probably part of the bumper tearing off, as the car shuddered to a stop.

But at least she was safe, she realized, when she was able to collect herself. No antelope had crushed her front end. The motor had died, but it started up when she put the car back in gear and started the ignition.

"Thank God."

She was thinking she should get out and check the damage when she caught a glimpse of the pronghorn in her rearview mirror. Standing alertly for a moment before leaping the barrier to disappear, the animal possessed glittering eyes that seemed to glow red…like the yellow coyote's.

Sorcery?

Except this time Mara had no way to escape, no Luke waiting for her to hang on to. Real fear chilled her, icy fingers jabbing their way up and down her spine.

Sorcery is sometimes real, sometimes illusion.

Like the pronghorn, this thought came out of nowhere.

And Mara took note. Logic sank in. She must have driven at least ten miles since the last pronghorn appearance. Though fast for short distances, such an animal couldn't have traveled this far. Or else some evil-intentioned person had a whole herd at his disposal.

Thinking illusion seemed more likely than reality, she pulled the car out and drove away. Something else clunked. More bumper? Not that she intended to stop and find out.

Fear was eclipsed by cool anger as she drove. Someone had tried to kill her. Someone was guilty... and had probably been standing around listening when she'd talked with Luke at Rebecca's house.

Unless the culprit was Luke himself.

But she didn't think so, didn't feel so in her heart. No matter how much he'd tried to make her doubt.

A sign appeared, announcing she was thirty miles from Santa Fe. She couldn't wait.

Rounding another curve, she saw the pronghorn appear up ahead again. Bounding straight down the middle of the road, the animal was headed directly for her windshield.

Illusion!

She repeated the word and muttered others, braced herself, kept her foot steady on the accelerator. She tried not to flinch, even as the animal came closer, closer, even as she stared into its spooky eyes.

The creature launched itself, sailed through the air... but there was no impact.

No impact!

She'd been right about it being an illusion.

A smile trembling on her lips, Mara drove on, encountering no more incidents on the way back to Santa Fe.

But maybe the evil person, whoever he was, knew she was a force to reckon with.

CHAPTER ELEVEN

"Mara Fitgerald, there you are."

Slightly disoriented by her mood—and the loud voices and the sound of flute music coming from the center of the courtyard outside—Mara turned to face the woman who was shouldering her way through a sea of bodies. A large woman with a commanding presence, Betty Sue Whitman made no bones about her love affair with everything Western. She was decked out in appropriate gear, from her hand-tooled snakeskin boots to her white Stetson looped with silver conchs.

"Mrs. Whitman, how nice to see you." Mara forced a smile to her lips, this regular customer's enthusiasm making it a bit easier. "I'm so glad you could come."

"Now, sugar, would I miss a Naha opening?" Mrs. Whitman waved a hand bedecked with several silver and turquoise bracelets and matching rings. "Not on your life."

Her life. Distracted from the festivities once more, Mara thought about the several days that had gone by without Isabel's training working for her. She'd made a prayer stick of wood and feathers, had painted it blue. She'd tried saying sacred words, concentrating on her breathing and her surroundings, but she hadn't been able to call up a vision if her life depended on it. Which it might. She hardly felt like a force to be reckoned with now. If she had any special powers, they were certainly well hidden.

She and Luke hadn't even shared another dream.

Nevertheless, Mara put on a good face for Mrs. Whitman's sake. "Can I get you a glass of champagne?"

"That would be lovely, sugar. You'll have one, too, I hope."

"If I had a drink with each of my valued customers, I would be a bit too tipsy to attend to business."

As they headed for a table where Felice was pouring the bubbly, Mrs. Whitman guffawed and whomped Mara on the shoulder. "You deserve to celebrate. I can't remember when I've seen such a successful opening."

Though Mara was certain the woman was exaggerating to be kind, she smiled and handed her a glass. "There are a couple of waiters passing around hors d'oeuvres."

"Heck, I don't need food. Let me at what's left of those new paintings so I can pick one out before some gaggle-eyed tenderfoot beats me to it." Mrs. Whitman winked and charged into the crowd.

And before Mara's mind could drift away again, Felice excitedly whispered, "I made *another* sale."

"Great."

The only thing that would have been better was if the artist himself were here to work the crowd. But she doubted that Luke could find it in himself to act civil to people in such a situation.

He couldn't even be civil with her. He'd acted very aloof toward her since the day Rebecca had died.

"People are going crazy over those newest pieces Naha did in acrylics," Felice was saying. "Only a couple are left."

Pieces done since the turmoil began at the pueblo, Mara knew. Luke's heightened emotions had affected his work, the results reflecting his darker moods. His work had moved to a new level, one that art lovers appreciated, as proven by the many Sold signs affixed to a good number of the paintings.

Mara told Felice, "I think I'd better circulate," then drifted off toward what was for her one of the most compelling pieces Luke had ever created.

Harbinger.

She gazed at what was another night view of the cliff and pueblo below. But it was the turbulent sky above that transfixed her. The very air was charged, alive as if with danger. Staring at the swirls and dips that formed movement across the canvas, movement from which a small figure was running, she could almost hear an ominous rumble that struck fear in her heart...almost as if she'd been there when something terrible had happened—a feeling far stronger than any of Luke's previous works had evoked in her.

"Naha's work is truly compelling, isn't it?" the woman next to her was saying to a friend about the very same piece.

"It's haunting," returned the second, popping a canapé into her mouth and washing it down with a sip of champagne.

"Fierce," the first murmured. "Unforgettable."

Like the man himself, Mara thought, shaking off the feeling that part of her was in another world. She was about to step back into reality, hopefully to make another sale, when an excited murmur set through the throng behind her. Mara turned to see what the commotion was about.

The crowd parted, revealing the artist himself, who was carrying two more finished paintings. Her gaze on the canvases, neither of which was framed, heart bumping against her ribs at the very sight of him, Mara moved toward Luke. But before she could get to him, he was mobbed.

And Betty Sue Whitman got her hands on both canvases. "Hot off the artist's easel. I got dibs on both of these, sugar, and damn the cost. Old J.D. can afford it, anyhow," she enthused, referring to her wealthy oilman husband.

Luke's penetrating gaze found Mara for a moment before she was swept along with the tide of excitement. She firmed up the sale with Mrs. Whitman, who wanted the paintings as is, refusing to leave them even long enough to be framed. Mara gave the new works the quickest of lookovers as she priced them, noting they were different views of the same cliff dwelling with night coming on. Though the red glow inside the structure seemed to be getting brighter, the sky above more restless. But the paintings disappeared before Mara could examine them more closely.

She was also frustrated in her attempts to stay close to Luke, who was dressed in black slacks, a black-on-black embroidered Western shirt and a silver-and-jet black pendant with a medicine-bear fetish. His long hair was free of the customary leather tie, hanging loose and sexy to frame his rugged features. Several women were giving him the eye and flirting with him. And Mara was amazed that Luke was actually acting polite, if not overly enthusiastic toward all the opening's attendees who wished to talk to him.

Just as he'd been polite—if aloof—toward her the past few days.

People stormed Luke for the next hour or so, while she and Felice were both kept busy writing up more sales. Mara tried to keep her mind on the opening's success, rather than on the artist himself.

Only after the crowd abated did Mara get anywhere near Luke.

"I didn't think you were going to show," she admitted, quickly adding, "but I'm really glad you did."

"Because you made extra sales?"

His acerbic tone and typical cynicism made her stiffen. "If that's what you want to think."

Mara started to walk away from him, but was stopped cold by his stepping in front of her. His nearness made her catch her breath. She couldn't control her physical reaction to him, no matter how hard she tried.

"Sorry." Then he spoiled the simple apology she was willing to take by adding, "I promised Mother and Grandmother that I would behave."

"And you wouldn't want to disappoint *them*."

He heaved a sigh. "I'm not good at nice words, okay?"

She bit back another sharp response. "Okay."

"Good."

His slow, steady smile got to her, as did the sudden feeling that he was on his best behavior for *her* alone.

Telling herself she must be crazy—Luke Naha had no feelings other than lust where she was concerned—Mara swallowed hard and forced out, "Champagne. It's your reception and you haven't even had a glass."

"I'll stick to soda, if you have it."

Warmth crept up her neck as she remembered why Luke didn't drink. "I'll get you one. And some appetizers."

To her surprise, their truce held for the rest of the evening, until every last prospective customer left. Because Felice had been putting in extra work for her while she'd been at the pueblo, Mara told the young woman to leave, as well, that she would do the cleanup.

"You don't mind being alone locking up?" Felice gave Luke an intense look. "Uh, I guess you won't be alone, huh?"

"I'll see that she's safe," Luke assured the woman.

A promise Mara wasn't certain Luke could keep in the bigger scheme of things, try as he might.

As he helped her trash plastic cups and paper plates and napkins, she asked, "How are things going at the pueblo? Made any breakthroughs?" She knew he'd been having as difficult a time as she summoning up a vision.

"Not yet. I've been thinking about building a sweat lodge. Maybe if I fast and meditate for as long as it takes... Hell, I don't know that it'll do any good, either. I don't understand how we could drift so easily into shared dreams, yet not come up with any visions of wisdom."

"Maybe you need another approach." Thinking of the power waiting to explode off his latest canvases, she suggested, "Maybe you should paint your nightmares."

"I told you—"

"I know what you told me. But something about your new work is different. More powerful. I think the nightmares are trying to come through. Maybe you have to release them before you can find the positive energy necessary to do what your grandmother asks of you."

"And what about you? Are you going to paint your nightmares, too?"

She hadn't thought of that. Hadn't even taken a brush to canvas in years.

"I don't know.... Maybe I should."

She knew she had neither the talent nor the power to match whatever Luke could create. And, unlike Luke, her nightmares and guilt came from two different directions. As far as she could tell, her chase dreams had nothing to do with the suicidal patient who'd begged her to enter his dreams before she was aware that she actually might be able to do so.

After sweeping up in the gallery and wiping off all the horizontal surfaces, they gathered leftover champagne and cans of soda. Their hands collided as they reached for the same bottle of bubbly. The small contact was enough to make Mara yearn for more, tempted her into making it happen. But in the end, her sense of self-worth won out and she took an armful of bottles and cans into her office. Luke followed with more. They set the extras on a credenza.

Then, disappointed that they'd finished so quickly, that she would have to take her leave of Luke so soon, Mara said lightly, "That about does it."

"For the opening."

About to filch her shoulder bag from the drawer of her desk, Mara hesitated. She knuckled the grained wood nervously. "Thanks for the help."

"You, too."

Staring into his serious gaze, which for once was neither hostile nor filled with hot desire for her, Mara knew Luke referred to her good intentions toward his people.

"I only hope I really can help, Luke."

He moved closer, brushed the backs of his fingers across her cheek, sending a tremor of longing through her.

"Whatever happens," he murmured, "I just want you to know that I've never met anyone as selfless as you, Mara."

She flushed and her pulse sped up. The longing intensified. She wanted to tell Luke not to stop, to keep touching her forever.

Instead, she whispered, "Of course you have. Your grandmother and mother are selfless. Rebecca was," she said, still as saddened by the wisewoman's death as she had been at her funeral. "And I'm sure you could name dozens of others. Most people have good in them."

"But most aren't willing to put their own life in danger for others who mean nothing to them."

The way Luke was staring at her so openly, so admiringly, gave Mara hope. If he could be this sincere with her now, even for a few precious moments, then perhaps he could someday leave all of his anger behind.

"But the Kisi do mean something to me," she said, touching his cheek in turn. Something that went deeper than she could express. "As do you."

"I care about you, too, Mara," Luke said, surrounding her with his arms.

Mara wondered if she were dreaming. She'd been waiting for what seemed like forever for Luke to admit to something more than *want* where she was concerned. At the moment, *care* seemed the perfect step forward.

And so when Luke pulled her closer, she didn't resist. She allowed herself to flow against him. Allowed her arms to snake around his neck. Their closeness seemed so right—far more familiar than was possible in the heartbeat of time that they'd known one another.

Her breath came quick and shallow as she anticipated his kiss.

Luke didn't disappoint. In a flash, he covered her lips and plunged his tongue deep inside her mouth. Heat lightning seared her as Mara imagined the rhythm of their mouths being that of a more intimate lovemaking.

Her lower body responded, hips instinctively moving in that same hypnotic rhythm. Without breaking their connection, he slid a hand down her thigh, hooked her behind the knee and tugged until she slid her leg up and around his hip. Pressing her against the desk, he stroked her body with his through the gauze of her Western-style dress, leaving her no doubts that even the obstructed contact affected him deeply.

It was as if, though fully clothed, they were already making love.

And when he backed off for a moment, his chest shuddering as he sucked in some air, it was her turn to say, "I want you, Luke."

His eyes locked with hers in silent question, as though he needed to be certain. Her answer was given in equal, heart-pounding silence.

With a groan, he buried his face in her neck, his lips and tongue teasing her sensitive skin. He freed a hand to slip under her skirt, to tear at the lace keeping her from him. She felt the delicate material give way...and his hand taking its place.

She was already hot and wet and throbbing for him. He slid two fingers along her most tender flesh, continuing until they were lost inside her. Unable to help herself, she picked up the rhythm once more, moving against his fingers even while wanting more of him.

Wanting a part of him that was somehow familiar...and yet not.

Feverishly, she tore at his belt and trousers.

Desperately, she released him.

Greedily, she pulled him toward her, until Luke was able to substitute one source of pleasure for another without missing a beat.

A beat that echoed through her conscious mind and drove deeper, calling to a part of her that she could not name. She'd done this before. Made love with him. She was certain.

But when?

"Mara."

Her name muffled against her throat sounded incredibly sensual, a promise met by Luke's lips as they traveled upward, once more finding her mouth. He pressed her harder against the desk, long enough to capture her free leg and seduce it upward as he had the first.

She surrounded him.

He invaded her.

Invasion.

War.

But surely not, for they were making love. They did love each other. She remembered...

Then, tightening his grasp on her and stepping back, Luke took all of her weight, his hands, his wonderful hands, cradling her buttocks.

Moving her.

Driving her.

Guiding her to ecstasy.

Only when Mara shuddered her release did he pause for a moment, whirling with her, heading her in a new direction. He found the couch and laid her back without losing her. Her breath came in gasps and her hands shook as she stroked his hair, his face, his shoulders.

"Hang on," Luke growled, driving deeper into her.

Thud, thud, thud. Thud, thud, thud.

The transition from thought to memory was a subtle shift.

Panicked, heart beating hard in her breast, she chanced a glance behind her...and saw someone, something horrible approaching....

He thrust again and again, each movement coming faster than the last. Mara felt the familiar pressure building. Panting, needing, she lifted her hips higher, grabbed his hair and brought his head down to her breasts. He sucked at her through the layers of material, used his teeth to tighten her nipples almost painfully.

As tension escalated to the unbearable, a cry started at the back of her throat.

She cried out and raised an arm to protect herself, but her killer did not stop. He wanted her dead....

She cried out again....

Luke captured the sound with another deep, hungry kiss, seconds later stiffening and echoing her feral sound.

They shuddered together, quakes becoming after-shocks.

And Mara lay under Luke...satiated...and stunned beyond words.

Isabel first prayed for Rebecca. Then she prayed for herself and for the Kisi people. She asked for guidance. For the protection of her ancestors.

Her hand trembled as she touched the feathered serpent, the snake kachina, which sat on the draped table in her bedroom. Then she climbed into her narrow bed, wondering if this would be the night she would not wake from her sleep. For as if the evil were a living, breathing thing, she felt its presence closing in around her.

What could she do?

She was old. And now she was alone. She was trying to pass on her knowledge to Mara and Stormdancer, but so far the effort had been an exercise in futility.

Perhaps if she did not sleep...

But she *was* old. And very, very tired. And try as she might, she could neither keep her eyes from closing nor her spirit from dreamseeking....

She floated into her dreaming place, an ancient rock formation, a deep red cliff that she had loved long and well. Herein lay her only safety.

Darkness gradually gave way to dawn, the first fingers of light tracing crimson patterns over the dry earth and rock, and painting with a blue luster the distant mountains, all of which had forever been a part of her world.

Silence, long and deep, but for the howling wind.

Suddenly, her insides brushed with fear.

Her eyes flashed open and, oddly, she saw all before her as if she were a stranger.

Desolate...forbidding...ghostly...rough-cut rocks weathered and wrinkled...the ends of the earth...unfit for human habitation. Above, the sky shifted. Gray and purple clouds rolled in, swallowing the newly weaned sun.

The wind howled...or was it a voice calling her name?

Corn Woman!

Lightning split both sky and earth.

She turned to see a dark shadow invading her space. A terrible shadow that was at once formless yet threatening. Evil. Her eyes widened in horror.

"Who are you?" Her hollow voice rode on the wind. Her heart beat like a drum. "Who are you?" she shouted again, even knowing death was stalking her.

With a cry, she plunged upward and her legs impelled her forward...away from her beloved dreaming place...seeking safety where there was none. The hard-packed earth and stones grazed her bare feet. Around her, translucent canyon walls zoomed by faster and faster until they were nothing more than a blur.

And then she felt them—the hands around her throat. But whose? She whipped around this way and that, trying to see, trying to identify the monster who would surely kill first her and then her people. But the evil remained out of sight, out of reach. Choking her.

Choking her land and then her people. Because before her very eyes the evil settled over the canyon and rocks, earth and sky, suffocating the plants and small animals that withered and died before her, stealing the precious light of life, replacing it with a darkness from which there was no escape for anyone.

She was old and not afraid to die, but once gone, she could not help the others.

Her pounding heart and rasping breath resonated through her head as she saw the world around her go dark and struggled against it. The band around her throat tightened, tightened, cutting off her air. She knew her struggle was useless, that she could not save herself.

Then, "Isabel!" came a familiar voice, giving her one last glimmer of hope....

"Isabel!"

Mara plunged upward, clutching her sheet. She was wet and shaking with fear. Dear God, someone—some *thing*—had been trying to get to Isabel. She'd gone dreamwalking again, and she'd seen it all.

"Luke?"

But he was gone. He'd seen her home and then had returned to the pueblo to guard Onida and Isabel.

The evil had slipped by him.

Without stopping to think about what she should or should not do, whether or not she should call Luke and find out what he knew or didn't, she threw on her clothes, grabbed her keys and ran out the door to see for herself.

Unwarned, he couldn't stop her.

Had he known, Luke wouldn't have let Mara come. How could he protect her? He couldn't even protect his own grandmother any more than he'd protected his wife and child.

Maybe he was the one, the doubt in him whispered. He'd been sound asleep. Who knew what evil he had dreamed? Maybe he'd done it...almost killed the fragile woman who'd never harmed a living thing.

"You're sure you're all right?" Mara was saying, holding his grandmother's hand. She glanced at him, gave him a brave smile.

He stiffened.

Onida stood on the other side of the bed, hands fluttering around her face.

Isabel said, "I am alive...only because you came when I needed you, Mara. I knew you could do it. I knew."

Mara had saved his grandmother. From him?

"Tell me about it, Isabel," Mara urged.

Tightening his jaw against the grief he couldn't express, Luke backed out of the room, leaving the three women to console each other. Three women with whom he had a special relationship.

His mother and grandmother had always been there for him, had believed the best of him. Now Mara. His making love with her in reality had changed things between them. They were bonded in a way he didn't understand and couldn't explain. He only knew that his feelings went deeper than he thought possible and were as scary as the dreams that had haunted him all his life.

He returned to his quarters, stared at the unfinished painting on the easel and at another stacked against the wall. More dark views of the mysterious cliff dwelling.

He sat. Tried to concentrate. To meditate using his paintings, for that seemed to be where the truth lay for him.

He had to know the unvarnished truth once and for all.

And there was only one way he could figure to get it.

He set aside the unfinished painting and set a clean canvas in its place.

Then he started painting his nightmares.

CHAPTER TWELVE

Chilled by Isabel's retelling of her nightmare, Mara renewed her determination to tap her inner resources, to find the power that the wisewoman believed she possessed. The burden of responsibility weighed heavily on her shoulders. She hadn't been able to stop the unnatural death of her patient, but she wasn't going to let Luke's grandmother slip away from them, as well, not while breath was left in her.

"In the morning," Mara told Isabel, "I'll be ready to try again. In the meantime, you should sleep."

Sitting on the edge of her bed, the elderly woman appeared exhausted and even more frail than usual, and yet she protested. "No. I must stay awake at night and sleep during the day. Perhaps by doing the unexpected, I can fool the witch who would see me dead."

"I'll sit here with you, then." Mara glanced at Luke's mother, who seemed grief stricken and helpless at the same time. "It's all right," she told Onida. "I won't let anything happen to Isabel now." She said it with more conviction than she was actually feeling. "And if she sleeps during the day, she'll need you to guard her."

Nodding, Onida hugged Isabel and touched her cheek lovingly. To Mara, she said, "I'll go to my bed, then, but you must call me if I'm needed."

"I promise."

Feeling the weight of that promise on her shoulders, Mara again wondered why Luke had disappeared within minutes of her arrival. Where could he be and what was he up to? Blaming himself again? Now that they'd made love, she felt closer to him than to any human being. What they'd shared went beyond a normal relationship. She had to help his family and his people ... for him.

After Onida left the room, Isabel sighed and lay back against her pillows. "You have the gift, as was proven again tonight. I do not understand why my training has so far been unsuccessful. At dawn, you must leave the pueblo without food ... go into the desert ... seek power in nature."

"But what if—?" Mara didn't want to admit that she feared failure. "For how long?" she asked instead.

Isabel turned her sightless eyes on Mara. "For as long as it takes. You must find your own dreaming place."

At a loss, Mara asked, "Where do I look? Which direction do I take?"

"Let instinct guide you. Allow yourself to let go of the real world, to seek on a higher plane. When you encounter your dreaming place, you will recognize it. Then you must fast and remain sleepless until you know why this particular spot is meaningful to you."

The whole process could take days, Mara realized, knowing she had no choice, despite the fact that it would interrupt her life. Before starting off, she would leave a message for Felice on the gallery answering machine. She would ask her assistant to take over for her and to assure Felice that she would somehow make up for this extra burden.

Chilled again by the realization of what she might be up against, Mara only hoped that she would be able to keep all her promises.

"Who knows what you'll have to deal with out there?" Luke groused when he finally faced Mara just before dawn. "I'm going with you."

He'd stayed up all night to complete a canvas that still held no definitive answers for him. Then, haggard, drawn and thinking he was emotionally spent, he'd come into the kitchen for something to drink, only to find Mara at the sink, filling a gourd with water. When she revealed her plans to storm the desert alone and on foot at first light, his emotions resurfaced fast enough.

"No, you can't come with me," she said stubbornly. "Isabel told me I must go alone. If you're around to distract me, I'll never find my dreaming place."

Distract her. Even fatigued and irritable as he was, the idea held a certain appeal. And he probably could do it, too. The chemistry between them was cooking even now. Watching her nervously lick her lips knotted him up inside and out. Making love once definitely had not been enough to satiate him even for half a day.

He moved closer, watched Mara's eyes widen, heard the sudden expectant intake of her breath.

Exhaustion dropped from Luke like a disguarded mantle. He shot out a hand and wrapped it around the back of her neck. She didn't resist but allowed him to draw her closer, her gaze searching and pleading at the same time.

Pleading for his kiss? His love?

Or pleading for him to let her go—the one thing Luke couldn't do.

He couldn't stop himself. With the water gourd between them preventing further intimacies, he kissed Mara, consumed her as if there were no tomorrow. Which there might not be if she persisted in taking on the high desert alone. But even as he recognized the danger, he also recognized the truth of his grandmother's words about Mara's needing to be alone to find her dreaming place.

And he recognized the importance of her doing so, and fast.

For if they each didn't make the supreme effort to reach a higher spiritual plane, his grandmother would surely suffer. Perhaps die. Then, no doubt, would the Kisi.

And Mara, whispered an inner voice that reminded him of the coyotes sent to track her down through witchcraft.

Why Mara? Why a white woman?

The answer still eluded him, as did the identity of the evil one . . . perhaps himself.

Savoring the taste of her mouth—an experience that would have to last him awhile—Luke lost himself for a moment more before releasing her. Then he drew back and memorized her face, every nuance of her expression. Her feelings for him—raw, deep, hungry—were written for him to see. He wondered if she saw the same in him.

"Be careful," he said, reaching around her and drawing a brimmed straw hat from a peg. "And wear this."

Taking a big breath, fastening the prayer stick she'd made to her belt and clutching a water gourd to her breast, Mara took the hat and edged away, her gaze never leaving his. "This has to work." She paused at the door. "I'll give it everything I have."

"That's all anyone can ask of another human being."

Luke watched her go. Fear for her tore him up inside, and he knew that a part of him went with her. He was beginning to suspect that he more than cared for the woman. If anything happened to her...

Only when she disappeared from sight did he close the door and return to his studio. Setting another blank canvas on the easel and taking up a brush, he determined to concentrate as hard as Mara would out on the desert.

Surely between them they would find some answers.

Answers didn't come easily, not even in the desert.

Having walked and searched for several hours, Mara sat beneath one of several cottonwoods lining a ribbonlike stream that trickled along a pebble-strewn path. The shade was a welcome respite from the sun, which had been high overhead for a while now. She uncorked the gourd and sipped at the refreshing water, thinking she should refill the half-empty vessel before moving on. Not having water in the desert—even in the cooler high desert—was asking for trouble.

Leaning back against the tree trunk, staring at the red earth and the red rock still a short distance away, she felt more alone than she ever had before. Alone but somehow at peace, as if she were one with the land.

The near-sleepless night caught up to her and her eyes fluttered, her mind drifted.

"You are putting us all in danger," intoned the elder, the very same woman who'd complained to her before. *"We are at war!"*

Her temper surfaced at the unnecessary reminder of the conflict that embroiled the Pueblos with the bloodthirsty Spanish. She stopped weaving the new cloth and kept her eyes lowered only with difficulty.

"He is not one of the cursed Spaniards. He is Comanche."

"Still you meet him in secret outside the protection of the pueblo—"

"My business."

"And your husband's."

"An old man to whom I was given by my family."

"And to whom you owe your respect."

She finally raised her eyes to the elder, stared at the seamed face so full of wisdom and wondered that she didn't understand.

"I do respect him and care about him in my own way. But surely," she pleaded desperately, *"you remember what it is like to really love...."*

Mara started. She hadn't been quite asleep, and yet the dream had invaded her mind. Or *was* it a dream? The threat of war and love lost had seemed so real...almost seemed like a memory.

Her hands shook as she lifted the gourd to her lips for a long draft of water.

A memory.

How many times had she been aware of the sense of cognition since setting foot on Kisi land? How many things had seemed familiar to her?

Mara stirred from her resting spot and refilled her container. Perhaps when she found her dreaming place she would also encounter the truth about herself. The thought filled her with both relief and dread. She set off, her feet automatically taking her past the Red Mesa, where she had first enountered Isabel in a dream.

But halfway through the afternoon, when she arrived at the floor of the canyon, no special feeling nudged her.

And so, on she went, hoping, praying that this time she would not fail. Instinct took her straight to the other side of the canyon from which there was no exit.

Or so it seemed.

Mara studied the series of boulders before her and realized there was a possible pathway between them. She drew closer, followed the intricate winding trail and came to a fairly large open area where she confronted a cleft in the rock face large enough for two men to ride through abreast.

Ride, not walk.

Spooked, she hesitated, her mounting apprehension keeping her from investigating immediately. Instead, she sank into the shade of a boulder and nursed another drink of water while staring at the inviting opening.

The rocks blurred before her tired eyes....

"You should not have followed me," she angrily told her lover. *"This entrance to the pueblo is secret."*

An errant breeze whirled through the opening, blowing his loose black hair around his face, as if he were about to fly away forever...her biggest fear.

"And who would I tell?" he demanded harshly. Then his voice softened. *"But I can use it to come to you."*

She nearly swooned with the desire his promise kindled in her. *"No, it's too dangerous for you."* The men of her pueblo would surely kill him if they were caught together.

"Then come away with me so we can be as one always."

Her heart ached to do just that, but she had her parents to think of, and her sisters and their children. She even considered her husband, for whom she had only a daughterly affection. *"I can't leave my people."* To never see them again would kill her.

"Because you don't love me."

"That's not true." Passionately, she cried, *"I swear to love you and only you until the end of time...."*

The vision or memory, or whatever it was, faded. Yet a sadness swept through Mara so great that it pinned her against the jagged rock. And tears that she couldn't control streamed down her cheeks. Grief? She'd experienced the same grief recently, after one of her dreams.

She stared at the cleft dividing the rock face, wondering what waited for her on the other side of the corridor.

Like a woman hypnotized, she rose and sought her present, and perhaps her past. As she entered the passageway, her pulse raced, dizzying emotions leaving her lightheaded. She hadn't had such strong feelings since setting out from Luke's house.

Luke. Where did he fit in?

He and the warrior seemed entwined somehow.

She was becoming as obsessed with Luke as the Kisi woman had been with her Comanche lover in the past.

The farther Mara went along the curving pathway, the more emotions swept through her. For Luke. For Isabel. For the Kisi. For the lovers whom she was certain had come to a tragic end.

Mara came to the end of the passageway and could see a clearing before her. Her throat tightened and the sound of her heartbeat thundered through her ears. She took one step into the clearing, sucked in a painful breath and squinted against the setting sun that painted the entire area with such a brilliant red it looked as if the rock itself were on fire.

Fire...

She stood there, eyes blinking, chest heaving, and waited for her pulse to steady.

Then, finally, struggling with apprehension, Mara raised her eyes. They widened as her gaze met the pueblo ruin built high into the rock—the very same cliff dwelling that had been haunting Luke's newest paintings.

And she was swept up by a feeling so strong she could not deny it, pulling her up the rocky slope toward a side entrance to the pueblo ruins. This was it. She was certain, just as Isabel had said she would be. She could feel the pulse of the very earth beat below her feet.

At last, she'd found her dreaming place.

Rubbing at his gritty, sleep-robbed eyes, Luke relieved his mother and sat watching his grandmother in her narrow bed, wondering if Mara had had any success in her quest. She'd been gone all day.

Her absence stretched into forever.

"I sense you are grieving, Stormdancer."

"Grandmother, you're awake." Luke breathed a sigh of relief as she sat up in bed. "And safe." For another day, at least.

She reached out and found his hand as easily as if she could see. "What is troubling you?"

"Everything. Mara."

His grandmother nodded. "She has not yet succeeded. At least my dreams were free of her presence."

And of any other presence, Luke assumed.

"Mara's probably as frustrated as I am. I'm sorry to let you down."

"You are still fighting yourself, Stormdancer. Open your mind, free it of what you know and seek what you do not."

Luke had felt he could do that with his paintings, that for him, his art was a substitute for a real dreaming place. He'd painted like a madman until he could no longer lift a brush. The horrific images he'd created in a near-hypnotic state had fired him into a frenzy, and yet he hadn't quite been able to leave the solid, earthly world behind. He'd gotten so far...and then had allowed something to pull him back.

Something called fear.

"I'm afraid our fate might rest on the shoulders of a white woman, Grandmother."

"Mara cannot do this alone. Only when the male and female are joined and work together can we reach our highest powers." She referred to the Kisi belief that both sexes needed to be involved for the highest sort of magic. "You must find a way to help her."

"And if I don't?"

His grandmother's silence spooked Luke. Her focus turned inward, away from him. But she didn't have to say the words.

Luke stood. "Should I send Mother in?"

"No. I will rise and eat now and stay on guard throughout the night. You are going to Mara?"

Luke hadn't put the urge to words, but he admitted, "I must find her." Noting the way his grandmother's lips tightened, he promised, "I won't disturb her from her mission. I only want to see that she's safe."

And he would have to force himself to stay awake, for, after what he'd created on canvas, who knew what kind of dream he might send her.

"Aie-e-e!"

Screams all around shuddered through her as she ran from the carnage. Spaniards had invaded the pueblo to surprise and overcome the men who had been unprepared for battle and the elders who hadn't had time to cast powerful protective spells. The scent of death and burning wood hung heavy on the early-morning desert air. But how had the Spanish soldiers gotten inside without alerting the guards? They must have come through the secret entrance.... Yet how had they found it?

Slipping and sliding down a slope toward the canyon floor, carrying her oldest sister's baby and holding the hand of her five-year-old nephew, she chanced a glance around and spotted him—her Comanche lover. Emerging from the flames, his face and body blackened with soot, a terrible burn scarring one arm, he flew after her, shouting her name, but two soldiers quickly restrained him. He struggled to no avail.

"No-o-o!" she cried, both a protest at his capture and at knowing why the walkways of the pueblo ran red.

Her lover had come for her, just as he'd threatened to do, and he must have been followed—that's how the Spaniards had gotten by the guards. She'd refused to give him up and so was responsible for the spilled blood of her people.

Her heart withered in her breast.

Her fault... all her fault.

Silent tears streamed down her face as the fire roared behind her. She had to save her sister's children. She started running, pulling along her small nephew when he began to wail. The baby in her arms whimpered. She shut out all sounds, especially those behind her—the pueblo falling in on itself and the death cries of those unlucky enough to still be inside. The Spanish soldiers would kill everyone except the younger women and the children big enough to work as slaves. If they caught her, the baby in her arms would die.

She wished she could die.

Somehow, she got safely to the canyon floor. Chancing one last look back at her lover, she saw a Spanish sword drive into the Comanche's heart. With an agonized shout, he fell to his knees... as did she. She clutched the baby to her breast so hard the little girl began crying.

As her lover died before her eyes, her mouth opened in a silent scream that went on and on, horror without end....

Sitting cross-legged amongst the ruins of the pueblo, Mara cradled her grief to her breast. This was no dream, but a memory of another life—she had seen other, older ones, including that of an Anasazi. But in this life, circa 1691, she had inadvertently betrayed her people, the Kisi. Tears seeped from her eyes and rolled down her cheeks.

Isabel had told her to learn why the place was so special to her, but Mara hadn't been prepared for the wellspring of pain the answers would bring.

She remembered being taken prisoner along with her nephew. Remembered being shackled with irons and chains, while the baby was abandoned, left alone to die under the desert sun. Remembered being introduced to the Spanish captain, Francisco Castillo, the pig whose sword had pierced her lover's heart—Luke's heart, she knew—and who was responsible for the death of her people.

No, she had been responsible, Mara reminded herself, as she floated once more....

The little girl's terrified wails haunted her as did her lover's death cry, even as she was reunited with what was left of the Kisi people. Her shame was so great, she couldn't speak to them again. She couldn't bear to feel their accusing eyes on her.

Silent for days, she plotted escape. She had nowhere to go, no plan but to die alone.

And then, when the guards became lax in their duties while they ate in front of her starving people, she took her chance. Still shackled, weak from hunger and thirst, she slithered silently between jagged rocks until she found a clear area along the mesa. Seeing her opening, she ran until she could run no more.

Head bowed under the beating sun, she stumbled along, barely able to move her heavy legs, even when she heard the pounding sound behind her.

Thud, thud, thud. Thud, thud, thud.

Something terrible was sweeping down upon her!

Fear put renewed speed to her legs.

The earth shook beneath her feet. Her pursuer was relentless, drawing loud, fiery breaths. A shadow loomed over her, cutting off the sun.

She was going to die!

She deserved to die, she thought, falling under the flashing hooves. Hot pain sluiced through her as the horse crushed her legs and hips, then her chest.

Capt. Francisco Castillo reining in his horse and grinning down at her was the last thing she saw before she died.

Weeping, Mara shook with guilt. She'd never meant to hurt anyone. She'd only meant to seek a bit of happiness with the man she loved. In that tragic life, she and Luke had been responsible for the Kisi being known as the *cursed ones*.

Suddenly other images swept the back of her closed eyelids. Other, newer lives, all as a white woman, in which love remained but a fleeting dream, her punishment for the lives lost in the Pueblo massacre. Now she realized she'd never had a truly satisfactory relationship, even in this lifetime. She was nearly thirty and had rarely considered marriage.

Through three centuries, she and Luke had renewed their roles as tragic lovers over and over again. But why?

Why were they still being punished?

It came to her that their present life finally gave them the chance to right the wrong for which she and Luke were responsible, a chance to save what was left of the Kisi people and remove the curse.

For her to do so, she had to be stronger than she'd ever been, Mara knew. She couldn't have doubts.

First she had to forgive herself.

Forgiveness did not come easy after what she'd witnessed. To be responsible for so many deaths was a horrible burden to bear. But she had only been human—*was* human. She concentrated. Prayed. Made a silent promise that this time she would not let her people die. For, though she had not been born a Kisi, Mara knew they *were* her people.

Time passed in a vacuum, but eventually she became aware of the invisible weight being lifted from her shoulders. Gradually, she breathed easier.

"I do forgive myself," she whispered to the night.

And the night breathed back, *This is good, Palo-Wuti.*

Palo-Wuti—somehow she knew that meant Snake-woman, and that it was her sacred name.

"Palo-Wuti." Repeating the name gave her a connection to the earth she'd never before felt. Connection and power. "Palo-Wuti."

Letting her mind drift once more, she found herself free of her corporeal body, floating above the pueblo, looking down on her semiconscious self. She heard sounds from miles around, sensed the creatures who inhabited the desert, and saw the exhausted man who slept behind a boulder below the cliff.

Luke had followed to protect her.

Luke, the man she loved, the man she had loved for more than three hundred years.

New tears streamed from her eyes when she opened them.

Stiff from sitting for so many hours, Mara rose slowly, testing her limbs as she straightened. She had to be with Luke right now. In the distance, the stars overhead were receding to await a new night. Dawn was almost upon them.

Climbing down from the pueblo, she came upon her lover's resting place. Rather than waking him, she sat on the earth nearby and watched him sleep, hoping that for the moment he was having only good dreams.

Mara now knew why nightmares about fire had invaded Luke's sleep all his life. Fire was a symbol of the pueblo burning, and especially all those lives lost because of his anger, his need to defy her and come after her, thereby giving unknowing entrance to the Spaniards who followed him. She wondered how long it would take Luke to face his guilt and come to terms with it.

Suddenly he stirred and made a sound deep in his throat. Her pulse picked up as she watched him wake. His eyes flew open and, startled, he sat straight up.

"Mara? What—? Is everything all right?"

Overflowing with excitement, she nodded. "I did it, Luke. I found my dreaming place."

"Grandmother will be relieved."

Rather than being openly happy for her, he seemed tense, and Mara knew he'd been unsuccessful in finding his own vision. She hesitated telling him the details of hers. In her heart, she felt that he had to discover the past for himself. That might be the only way he could deal with the horror, the only way he could forgive and believe in himself.

She stared at him through the eyes of a love older than she had ever thought possible. Thick hanks of black hair had worked free from the leather thong in back. She reached out a hand to touch the strands, then ripped the thong free. His hair fell around his face and, for a second, Mara saw her fierce Comanche warrior.

He grabbed her wrist, brought her palm first to his lips where he kissed it, then to his cheek where he cradled it as if it were precious.

"I'm glad you're safe," he said softly.

Her heart thundered. "Thank you for protecting me."

"I fell asleep—"

She slid her hand back over his mouth to stop him from blaming himself, something he did far too often. He kissed her tender flesh again, then removed the hand so he could draw her close. In a flash, Mara felt Luke's heart beat against her breasts ... the heartbeat of a passionate and jealous Comanche reborn as a shuttered and angry Kisi.

Then she savored his kiss—rough, hungry, consuming.

He cupped her breast, thumb circling her nipple, arousing her unbearably so that she moaned into his mouth. Burning with desire, she melted inside. She wanted him. Needed him. She always had. When his hand slid farther between them to undo the buttons of her shirt, she undid his with equal fervor.

In minutes, they lay naked upon the discarded clothing beneath a sky that had lightened to azure. She smoothed her hands over his bare, broad chest ... or was it that of her Comanche lover?

He was both.

"You fill my thoughts," Luke growled as he lay lightly upon her, taking both her wrists prisoner and lifting them above her head.

"And you mine."

She parted her legs and bent her knees, breath catching in her throat as she felt him probe her. As if destined, he found her heart without ever releasing her hands. She tilted her hips, easing his entry. She needed no readying for this moment. She'd been waiting for him for centuries.

Her heart beat an ancient rhythm, her soul recognizing his. She only hoped he could do the same and soon, for she longed to share the past with him openly.

But for now, as Luke drove into her, Mara welcomed the new day dawning...and a renewed hope for their future.

CHAPTER THIRTEEN

Mara's hope dimmed a bit when they arrived at the pueblo and found Isabel in her bed, damp with sweat and thrashing. Small, hoarse cries occasionally escaped her.

"She's been like this since she fell asleep at dawn," Onida said, wringing a wet cloth and placing it on Isabel's forehead. "I think she's sick from fighting the evil."

Guilt crept through Mara as she remembered what she and Luke had been doing at dawn. Then again, the walk, rather than their lovemaking, had kept them from home until midafternoon.

Luke gently took a frail hand in his. "Grandmother, can you hear me?"

"Stormdancer?" The sightless eyes opened. In a broken voice, Isabel said, "The Kisi are doomed. I have no strength left with which to fight."

"Then we will fight for you," Mara promised.

Luke gave her a startled look and shook his head.

But Mara ignored him and continued. "You leave it to Luke and me, Isabel. We'll take care of everything. I found my dreaming place."

"Then you found your visions?"

"Yes," Mara said as Luke's expression went from angry to furious. "Now you can truly rest. Sleep at peace, knowing that we'll work together to stop the evil from spreading."

"Good." Isabel's paper-thin lids fluttered over her eyes. "Good." She was instantly asleep, her body relaxed, her breathing deep.

"Thank goodness," Onida said. "I feared for her life."

"We all did." Mara glared at Luke.

"I need to see you outside," he said through gritted teeth.

"Perhaps your mother needs someone to take over for her a bit more."

"No, I'm fine." Onida's round face was wreathed in a relieved smile. "I'm glad your search in the desert turned out well, Mara." She turned to her son. "And your painting, Luke."

He patted his mother's arm but didn't respond. To Mara, he said, "Outside," in a steely tone.

This time she didn't argue, but followed him as he stormed out of the house. He was treating her as he had when they were still strangers. And making her equally angry. He didn't stop until he reached the small courtyard where she'd watched him paint the first time she'd come to the pueblo.

"What the hell is wrong with you—?"

"Isabel needed to rest easy," she said, cutting him off.

"With a lie?"

"A half-truth."

"What's the difference?"

"Why argue with me, Luke? Why not put some of this anger toward turning the half-truth into the whole truth?" she challenged him coldly. "You promised you would try."

"I *have* tried."

"Not hard enough." If she was being unfair, she didn't care. Too much was at stake for her to care.

"Who are you to say what is enough or not?" he demanded. "Maybe Grandmother was wrong and I'm not the one. Maybe there's nothing for me to learn."

Mara was tempted to tell him how wrong he was, but he had to face the past himself. "You don't believe that, Luke. Are you really so afraid of the truth? So much so that you would abandon your own grandmother, your own people?" *Her?*

His complexion darkened and his expression turned to stone. Mara waited for the explosion, but it didn't come. Instead, he spun on his heel and stalked away.

"Luke?"

He ignored her.

"Luke, wait, please."

And kept going . . .

"Luke."

. . . right through the gate.

"Damn!"

She felt like going after him, haranguing him until he agreed to put forth another, greater effort . . . but what good would that do? Despondent, she thought to relieve Onida, until she remembered the woman saying something about Luke's painting, as if she'd expected him to find his answers there.

For the past several days, he'd been working on scenes of the cliff dwelling. . . .

Curiosity led her to his studio even knowing Luke would probably be doubly angry about her entering it without his permission.

Shock pinned her to the spot the moment her gaze hit the three paintings lined up to dry against one wall.

Even from where she stood, the powerful images grabbed her.

Fire.

He'd done it. He'd taken her advice.

Luke had finally painted his nightmares.

Slowly, Mara inched closer to the first painting. Realizing the image was familiar, a sight that she'd seen in her vision, she gasped. For there on the canvas, the pueblo burned. Some tiny figures seemed to be trapped within the flames, while others fled in every direction. In the foreground was the silhouette of a woman holding one child's hand and pressing a baby to her breast.

Mara's heart thundered. Luke had painted *her* as part of his nightmare.

Her intent gaze quickly shot to the second painting, a closer look at the torched pueblo. Flames leaping off the canvas were so real, she had to take a deep breath and rub the gooseflesh from her arms.

But the third canvas held her riveted the longest. Now Luke had gotten inside the burning pueblo. Flames seared every surface—flames that, given a harder look, were in truth faces . . . tortured, horrified faces of the people who had died in that fire. She remembered her Comanche lover staggering out of the burning pueblo, his arm seared. He had been witness, then, to terrible sights.

Without fully realizing what he had done, Luke had painted something far more complex than simple nightmares—what were, in fact, his own macabre memories.

She didn't know how long she stood there, picking out those agonized faces one by one, inspecting them intently. Did she really recognize them or was she reaching? Could that be her mother? A neighbor? *Her husband?*

Mara was stunned. Luke had been so close. So very close. How could he have not realized that? How could he not have taken the last step?

He hadn't wanted to, an inner voice told her. His fear of himself was too great.

The art therapist in Mara surfaced. Rather than railing at Luke, she should have taken a firm, but more positive, approach. Backing off from the power that did, indeed, leap off the canvas, she determined to find Luke and convince him to try again. Offer to be with him when he sought the truth he'd shut out, if that would help.

She quickly checked the house, but he hadn't returned.

When she stepped outside to find him, she grew uneasy. She didn't think she'd been inside so long, but hours must have passed since they'd returned from the cliff dwelling, for the sky had darkened to a greenish gray, and a chill wind swept through the courtyard. The cottonwood quivered under the assault. The air was damp, signaling rain.

Odd . . . she didn't remember any storm warnings.

Rubbing some warmth into her arms, Mara jogged out of the yard and through the pueblo, alert for a glimpse of Luke. But all she saw were a couple of people heading into their houses and a dog skittering around a rusting car without any tires. She headed toward the pastures, wondering if he'd gone out to the desert again.

"Luke!" she called, to no avail.

No one answered. No one was around to hear. The pueblo appeared deserted, the vacant windows of the mud-brick buildings staring out at her like unseeing eyes, reminding her of Isabel's blindness . . . and vulnerability.

"Luke!" Her voice echoed hollowly into the fast-approaching night.

The abandoned feel of the pueblo spooked her, so that when thunder rolled in the distance, she jumped. Lightning quickly followed, cackling from the near-black sky, forking down to the silhouetted mesa in the distance.

Lightning Over Red Mesa.

Her pulse jagged as she stared out into the distance at the corruption of Luke's vision. Rather than magical, the vista appeared sinister. The very air around her felt heavy and menacing.

She was fatigued, imagining things, for the moment discouraged.

"Luke!" she yelled one last time.

Hearing nothing but the wind and the spatter of rain against dry earth, she headed back the way she'd come. Her bone-weary body was starting to protest. Her legs were heavy and she felt as if she carried a burden on her shoulders. She desperately needed sleep.

Perhaps her exhaustion was playing tricks on her, for suddenly she had the weirdest feeling she wasn't alone. A whisper on the wind rose the hair on the back of her neck and the flesh along her spine. Continuing faster toward Luke's home, she searched through the curtain of raindrops, but saw no one.

The whisper came again—a fluttering sound so light she might have imagined it. This time Mara turned her face up into the driving rain.

A large shadow loomed against the darkening sky— a bird with a wingspan of four or more feet. Startled when the horned owl seemed to come straight for her, she tripped and went down to her knees with a slight splash. Wet seeped through her clothing. Her breath came sharp, her heartbeat accelerated. Pressing her hands against the already-sodden sandy earth, she pushed off and ran for home.

Something soft and yet firm whacked her in the head. Hard. She ducked and glanced up to see the bird wing away and circle around, as though it meant to dive-bomb her again.

This was no accident, no freak of nature, Mara realized, beginning to shake from the damp and fear. First coyotes. Then pronghorn antelopes. Now a horned owl. The coyotes may or may not have been real. The antelopes had not been, as she had proved. This was no illusion. She'd felt the wing graze her. But an owl wouldn't normally attack a human any more than a coyote would.

Witchcraft!

Then how to fight it?

The brown-speckled owl opened its hooked beak and screeched at her, the belligerent sound skittering down her spine. Shuddering, she raised an arm to protect her head and to fight off the oncoming bird if necessary. The owl's wings fluttered as if in a braking motion, and its razor-sharp talons came straight for her.

Tensing all her muscles, ready to dodge the bird at the last second, Mara thought quickly. She swooped down toward the ground and with her free hand grabbed a hunk of wet earth, which she quickly pitched. The clod thunked the bird and rained sandy mud all over her.

The owl screeched indignantly, its wings rushing as it reconnoitered.

"Begone!" Mara yelled in Kisi without thinking, scooping up more cloying mud. "Evil, turn back on yourself... return to your sender!"

Her command was backed by another roll of thunder. The sky lit spookily, allowing her to see clearly as the bird shifted course away from her.

Mara pitched the second handful of wet earth. The clod's trajectory was perfect. The mud hit the owl's tail feathers as it flapped furiously away.

Then, wet and filthy, lump in her throat, chest squeezed tight, Mara ran for all she was worth, slipping and sliding over the wet ground but not stopping until she reached Luke's home. Heart pounding wildly, lungs feeling ready to burst, she threw open the kitchen door and tumbled inside, sinking to the floor in a loose-limbed puddle.

She didn't know how long she remained collapsed there, wet and shaking, before realizing she wasn't alone.

Barefoot and bare chested, hair loose and jeans riding low on his hips, Luke stood in the doorway, looking only half-awake and sexier than she'd ever seen him. He was staring at her, his expression grim.

"What happened?" he asked tightly.

A breath shuddered through her. "A horned owl attacked me."

"You're not hurt?"

If he was concerned, then why didn't he move toward her, help her off the floor, take her in his arms? Instead he remained frozen. Hostile? Certainly closed off.

Suddenly chilled inside, Mara got to her feet on her own steam. What in the hell was wrong with him? Why was he acting so peculiar?

"I was out looking for you," she said, trying not to make her statement sound like an accusation.

"We must have just missed each other. You were gone when I returned. I...fell asleep."

Drawing closer, she realized his expression wasn't hostile but haunted. Surely he didn't blame himself? Then again, a logical part of herself questioned, did he have reason to? Each time she'd been in danger, she'd been alone. Each time, Luke had some reason to be angry with her.

Surely not.

Still...

Not knowing what else to do, she stared at the floor and tried rushing by him, only to find her arm manacled by his hand. She stopped short.

"You're wet and cold."

She wouldn't tell him she was shivering more from the contact with him than from being rained on and attacked by an owl.

"You ought to get into a hot shower and into some dry clothes," he continued.

She tried to lighten the heavy atmosphere. "Like I packed a suitcase before I came."

"I can spare a T-shirt and cutoffs while your clothes dry."

The thought of Luke's clothes snug against her skin warmed Mara from the inside out. "Uh, thanks."

Just when she thought he would let her go, he roughly pulled her into his arms. She fought her qualms. She knew this man. She'd known him for longer than this lifetime—perhaps forever. He would never intentionally hurt her.

She stared up into his fathomless eyes and willed him to know her. To know himself.

And when he warmed her with a burning kiss, she thought surely he must realize the deep familiarity of the embrace.

Then, for a moment, she forgot everything but the present, the heady sensations she was experiencing pressed against his length. Her tongue met his in an explosion of desire. Her hands traveled over the smooth skin of his chest. His heat drugged her. Consumed her. She wanted nothing more than for him to lead her into his studio and make love to her amongst his visions on canvas.

Maybe then he would know her true name.

When he broke the kiss and led her to his wing of the house, she was convinced he meant to make love to her, especially when he dragged her into the bedroom. Her breath quickened, as did every nerve ending in her body.

Then he let go of her hand and, broad bronzed back to her, started rummaging through a chest of drawers. A moment later, he turned, holding a soft cotton T-shirt and washed-out denim cutoffs.

"Here," he said, handing her the clothing. And unnecessarily he pointed out the door to the bathroom. "Shower's in there."

"Coming with me?" She kept her tone light, hoping he would take her up on the invitation to shower together—to make love to her until nothing else mattered—but trying not to let him know exactly how much it would mean to her.

To her disappointment, he backed off and grabbed another T-shirt from an open drawer. "I'm going out to check and see what's going on around the pueblo."

Mara fought her warring emotions. Perhaps making love at the moment wasn't the best idea. Still, she already felt his loss.

"Be careful, Luke. I think the evil one is getting desperate." And he had not yet found his power. "When you get back, I'll be with Isabel."

Nodding, he slipped the T-shirt over his head, and Mara took the opportunity to escape into his bathroom. Once inside, she closed the door and pressed her back against the wood panel, straining to hear his every movement around the bedroom. Only when the soft scuffing faded did she approach the shower.

Perhaps with his grandmother's help, she could talk Luke into trying again, into seeking his spiritual self, into taking the final and most important step necessary to become whole at last. If only he could forgive himself, Mara prayed, she and Luke could surely stop the evil one before anyone else died.

Only then would they have a chance to make up for some of the lives lost because of their love that had been doomed over several lifetimes.

Doomed . . . he was a doomed man unless he acted shrewdly . . . and fast.

His dreams were totally out of control, haunted with scenes of blood and fire and death—visions that felt more like truth than fantasy. He had learned to fear sleep, for sleep had become his enemy.

But what to do?

Mara Fitzgerald was the one responsible for his terror. She was growing stronger and stronger while he was fast losing his mind. He'd seen *her* in his dreams and had recognized her true power.

He'd tried to scare her, to stop her by using Kisi magic, but she was clever. She had not buckled. Had not died. She had turned his magic against him.

If he didn't act fast, figure out a clever, diabolic way to stop her, *he* would be the one to die.

Death was uppermost on Luke's mind as he traversed the perimeters of the pueblo, looking for trouble in the unfathomable dark. Victor Martinez's death. Rebecca's death. Now both his grandmother and Mara were in danger. The question was, from whom? *Him?*

Mara had been attacked yet again by the doings of Kisi magic. He'd been asleep. Dreaming. Had he gathered the dark forces buried deep within himself and sent them after her in the form of an owl? He didn't know.

His boots squished against the wet sand. The rain had stopped and unless the skies reopened, the porous desert earth would soon be dry. A miracle of nature.

He needed a miracle.

He needed to see, for once unfettered by the blindness that went beyond his grandmother's handicap. Mara had been right to reproach him. Fear kept him from delving deeper within himself, for what if he did so and thereby unleashed a monster? Thinking about the third in his newest series of paintings, he concluded that only a monster could have created those horrific faces in the flames.

A monster whose nightmares were, in fact, truth.

Night had fallen. The air was still and cloying, and from the innermost reaches of his gut, Luke could sense evil rising around him…and could only hope the corruption didn't come from himself.

"Naha, there you are."

Luke would know that voice anywhere. "Looking for me, Mahooty?"

A light flashed in his face, and Luke sensed Charlie Mahooty wasn't alone. No doubt his slimy pal Delgado was with him.

"We've got you now, Naha," Mahooty stated. "Two witnesses are saying they saw you out by the community center an hour or so before it burned."

Luke stiffened. "The community center?" He'd dreamed about fire that night but hadn't thought he'd walked in his sleep, too.

Delgado snickered.

Mahooty went on. "Got a warrant for your arrest. You're some piece of work, Naha. Arson. Didn't want anybody else to enjoy your murals or something?"

The air around Luke wavered crazily. Was this solid proof that he could be lethal when he was sleeping? "If there are witnesses, why didn't they come forward before?"

"They were scared," said Delgado, moving closer to clamp metal around Luke's right wrist before he could react.

"But nobody's gonna have to be scared any longer. Lucas Naha, you're under arrest," Charlie Mahooty stated.

Delgado got hold of his other arm and twisted it behind his back. *Click.* He was handcuffed, unable to struggle, even if he wanted to. He didn't. Maybe this was best. Maybe he was finally going to suffer for his wrongs, even if a community center hardly compared to the lives of his wife and child.

Though he could still dream in jail, he worried. His arrest wouldn't necessarily make anyone safe....

"C'mon, get going." Delgado pushed at Luke, making him stumble forward. "We're gonna lock you up tight until the county sheriff arrives. Then we're turning you over. Arson'll get you a prison sentence. You won't be no danger to nothing and no one, at least for a while."

"What about my family?"

"Maybe if you cooperate, I'll tell your family where you are in the morning," Mahooty said.

Mahooty on one side, Delgado on the other, the two men held Luke's arms as though he might try to escape. He wouldn't. His only real regret was that he wouldn't get to say goodbye in person to the people he loved. His mother and grandmother. And Mara. Definitely Mara. He felt as if he'd loved her for more than a lifetime.

His thoughts caught up with losing the woman he loved, Luke didn't realize where the two men were taking him until they stopped in the middle of the plaza. The jail was still a hundred yards away.

"What's going on?" he asked.

"We're gonna make sure you can't ever interfere with my business again," Mahooty stated.

Delgado snickered.

And for the first time, as he heard the gun cock and felt the metal barrel press against his head, Luke realized he'd been a fool to go along with the thugs without a fight.

"Open the kiva," Mahooty told his cohort.

The sacred heart of the pueblo was a subterranean structure. Luke could only see Delgado's silhouette as the man rolled back the cover from the circular opening. Normally one entered or exited the kiva by ladder through this smoke hole for the fire that burned during ceremonies. But now Delgado pulled out the ladder, laid it on the ground and grabbed Luke's arm.

"Make sure he don't wake up too soon," Delgado told Mahooty.

For a second, the deadly gun was removed from Luke's temple. Then he heard it rush back toward him. He ducked. Still, metal met flesh again and again, and stars exploded inside Luke's head. He crumpled forward. As if he were observing from outside his body, he felt himself falling....

Luke awoke sometime later to a vacuum. Dark. Airless.

Where was he?

He shifted too quickly, and his throbbing head and battered body reminded him that Mahooty had thrown him down inside the kiva. Fearing something might be broken, he tested his limbs as best he could, considering his hands were bound behind him. Thankfully, everything more or less worked. Luke peered into the dark, wondering how long he'd been unconscious. Wondering how he would get out of this place. Wondering if his grandmother and mother and the woman he loved were all safe.

Hard to keep his thoughts straight when his head throbbed like a drum.

He lay back. Prayed for strength. And wisdom. For how long a time, he wasn't certain.

Gradually, he felt another presence.

He knew that in the floor of the kiva was the round, navel-like notch of the *sipapu*, symbolizing the place where humans had emerged from the earth, also thought to give spiritual access to yet another world deeper below. And from the wall behind the altar was a spirit tunnel. Pueblos had always accepted more than the corporeal state of being.

"Who's there?"

One who would have your help.

He imagined the words rather than actually *hearing* them, and yet the sender was familiar, had been since his youth. "Victor?" He didn't know why he called out, since Victor Martinez, the last of the storm-bringer priests, was dead, killed by the evil that plagued the pueblo.

Our people need you, Stormdancer. You must recognize your past before you can secure the Kisi's future.

No one but his grandmother had ever called him by the name he'd taken at manhood.

"What if *I* am the evil?" Or crazy? For he was talking to less than a shadow in the darkness.

You must dreamseek.

"I've tried."

You turned back from the truth too soon.

Mara had indicated as much. He whispered honestly, "But I'm afraid."

You must face your greatest fears and make peace with them, or the Kisi are doomed. Your woman cannot triumph over the evil alone. The most powerful medicine is made by a spiritual joining of the male and female. You are needed to make a future for our people possible.

Angrily, Luke cried, "There's too much darkness in me!"

But his words hollowly rang off the walls. Waiting for an answer, he was disappointed. The voice in his head had retreated, as if he'd driven it away.

"What should I do? How should I start?" he implored the dark, anyway.

The answer was his own, for Luke knew he had to begin with the visions he'd painted earlier that day. At last he was ready to face his nightmares. He had to allow himself to know the whole truth. To take a step beyond what he'd already seen.

He concentrated on fire, on the burning images that haunted his nights....

He was consumed with burning emotions.

Obsession for the woman who was his heart. Rage at being thwarted in his demands that she run away with him. Jealousy for the old man of a husband who had access to her bed anytime, day or night.

He had a mind of his own. He would not wait until she sought him out again.

He would go to her now....

Startled by the unexpected memory—for the emotions were so vivid and clear in his mind, Luke realized they had to be real—he wondered how his will had turned him from his course. What did lust and love have to do with his nightmares?

Fear kept him from wanting to find out, even as fear forced him to search further.

He easily found the secret entrance to the pueblo. Once known, it no longer had the power to hold her from him.

As his feet trod the rocky passageway that twisted this way and that, his heart thundered in his chest.

Soon he would see her. He would steal her away, and then they would be together always, just as they were meant to be.

He easily overpowered the single guard who amused himself with a solitary game of chance rather than seeing to his duty. The hidden entrance was thought to be secret and so did not require such careful scrutiny as did the frontal approach. He bound the man's hands and feet with leather thongs, used a wider strip of hide over his mouth—should the guard waken too soon, he could not alert his clan.

Then he ran for the main dwelling structure, only to hear scuffling and muffled voices and animal sounds behind him. Thinking more guards had been alerted, he threw a glance over his shoulder. To his horror, he saw other men pouring from the secret entrance. Men dressed in the clothing of the dreaded Spanish soldiers.

Some were mounted, all were armed, a few carried torches.

Torches. Fire . . .

One torched the nearest building, while the captain ran a sword through the unconscious and bound guard.

Bleeding inside with guilt, he ran, knowing he had led the enemy into the heart of the Kisi pueblo. He ran, thinking to save the woman he loved from the curse that his jealousy had brought down upon her people. . . .

And when the action had played itself out, Luke sat frozen in the dark, stunned, knowing that this had been no vision but a memory. If not for him, there would have been no fire, no horrible, haunting deaths. If not for him, the Kisi would never have been nearly decimated. If not for him, his people would not now be cursed.

Surely the darkness within him was more evil than he had ever imagined.

CHAPTER FOURTEEN

Mara's eyes flashed open to the dark, though she had no idea what woke her. She had slept a bit, but was still exhausted, still wearing Luke's T-shirt and cut-offs. She'd waited for his return for hours until Isabel finally had risen and ordered her to rest. She'd gone to Luke's room, had tried to pretend he was with her in his bed....

Turning on the lamp, she squinted at the clock. Nearly four a.m. If Luke had returned, he hadn't made himself known. And though she'd slept a few hours, she was getting a headache, the symptom of needing more rest, though she was no longer sleepy. She rose, moving carefully so as not to make the headache worse.

Barefoot, she padded out into the hall, intending to make some nice, soothing tea. But a voice called to her.

"Mara, come join me."

She entered the living room, dark but for several lit candles, illuminating sacred figures in their niches—kachinas and Catholic saints—and casting a spooky glow over the slight figure in the overstuffed chair. "Isabel, what are you doing here alone?"

"Onida needed her sleep. So did you."

"How are you feeling?"

"Better...yet worse." Shadows flickered across her face. "Luke... Something is wrong."

A chill shot through Mara. "He didn't come back, then."

"No. I fear for him."

As did she. Why hadn't she stopped him from leaving the house alone? As if she could stop him from doing anything he wanted, any more than she could force him into anything he didn't.

Rubbing at the back of her neck—this was some weird headache coming on—she assured Isabel, "Luke will be all right." He had to be.

"Then where is he?"

Mara shrugged, her attention taken over by the buzzing at the back of her skull. She'd had headaches in her day, but nothing like this. Tea wouldn't do a damned thing to ease this kind of pain. "My head feels like someone's pounding on it," she told Isabel. "I think I'd better find some aspirins."

But before Mara could leave the room, Isabel sucked in a loud breath and intoned, "White man's medicine cannot fix what is wrong with you."

Mara's hands flashed to her head. Damn if she didn't feel like someone was driving through her skull as if trying to get inside. "What do you mean?"

From a distance, she heard Isabel reply, "The evil is upon us."

The prayer stick Mara had made was lying in one of the niches. Without thinking, she picked it up and tried to focus on the wisewoman. But the room wavered. Isabel's face went out of focus. And the pounding at Mara's skull intensified.

The evil...

Flesh crawled up her spine and her blood rushed through her veins.

"What do I do?" she gasped.

"Fight it!" Isabel ordered, as if from a vacuum. "Fight the evil with everything you have learned!"

The buzzing at the back of her skull became unbearable. Horrified, Mara sank to the floor, clutched the prayer stick to her, closed her eyes and tried clearing her mind. She took deep, if shaky breaths.

She concentrated on her sacred name, Palo-Wuti...

... *and in her mind became Snakewoman.*

She stood on the earthen floor of a long narrow canyon, its walls so fiery the very brilliance of the red hurt her eyes. And the wind howled so fiercely around her, its whistle threatened to pierce her ears. Grasping her feathered prayer stick, straightening her posture, she pushed her discomfort away and concentrated on finding the one whose summons she had answered.

A prickling sensation at the back of her neck made her aware of a malevolent force behind her. Slowly, she turned, the deliberate action bringing her face-to-face with a red-eyed man, who was painted and feathered as intricately as any of Isabel's kachinas.

Hatred hit her like a hot wind and her heart thundered with a fright she tried to bury.

"Who are you?" she demanded, her voice trembling in spite of herself and echoing along the corridor. "What is it you want of me?"

"Call me Witchman." He laughed, the reverberation virulent. "Or perhaps you prefer my Kisi name—Lucas Naha. Such a foolish woman, thinking I wanted to change my ways. Thinking I might love you."

"Luke?" Heart pounding with dread, she concentrated on seeing beneath the disguise, concentrated on

learning his true identity, but she only succeeded in frustrating herself.

"You should have stayed away," he told her. "I betrayed you once and I'll betray you again, this time for good. Your death will amuse me."

A painted arm plunged up toward the sky, the hand opening and fisting in a gesture of power.

The winds instantly whirled in a circle around her. Overhead, ominous black clouds rolled in and the sky opened. Thunder barked its frightening laughter and heat lightning zapped the earth mere inches from where her feet were planted.

Was the man she loved really trying to kill her?

Despair deeper than she'd ever known gripped her. And for a second, she let her concentration slip.

Suddenly, she found herself rushing upward, the walls of the canyon striating, stretching, lengthening. The speed was dizzying, leaving her powerless. Then she was left standing atop a mesa, toes too close to the edge for comfort. Her insides clutched as she wavered. A laugh from behind startled her into carelessness. Turning awkwardly and too fast, she saw the painted arm coming for her. An open hand smacked her in the chest like a lightning bolt, its sizzling power plunging her over the rim.

"No-o-o!"

She plummeted, weeping that her lover could truly be so evil.

But there were other people to consider, a voice deep inside reminded her. Other people to protect.

As she quieted her emotions, she understood that Witchman was trying to scare her into dying in spirit so that her flesh would follow. And then she would be of help to no one. She concentrated on saving herself.

Instantly she was floating on a soft current that drew her in a different direction, giving her time to regroup, finally setting her down in the cliff dwelling that was her powerful dreaming place.

But the ghostly dwelling was filled with dark shadows, which meant Witchman had preceded her.

She searched the darkness for him, but found things that were far more subtle...a ghostly face suddenly bloomed in the shadows...a muted wail came from somewhere nearby.

Ghosts! People who had died in the massacre.

Her heart thudded as spectral bodies seemed to materialize before her eyes, limbs twisted and bloody, startled eyes open in horror.

The ghosts were restless, floating, wandering, gathering. They lurked in every corner.

Murderess! they accused, *their voices hollow.*

Guilt seized her, heart and soul. She wept, sobbing aloud.

But she realized she couldn't allow this. She had forgiven herself. She had another chance to right the wrong. But did she have the power to overcome the evil this time?

She wasn't certain she could do it alone.

The ghosts started fading...

Only to be replaced by a voice that echoed from every chamber. "I will enjoy killing you," Witchman growled, "along with the old crone you protect with all her drivel about Kisi magic."

"You would kill your own grandmother?" The grandmother her lover had professed to cherish? The elderly woman she was sure he did love? "I don't believe you!" One way or the other, Witchman was ly-

ing. Either he wouldn't kill his grandmother... or he wasn't who he said he was.

Witchman's laugh was pure evil. "When I get through with the Kisi, they won't be the cursed ones any longer. They'll be the ones who disappeared."

Clutching her prayer stick, she prayed for the truth and for help....

Both came in the form of someone suddenly approaching, bursting through the secret entrance. Snakewoman stared at the man as he ran toward her, his long hair flying behind him, his face bloody.

She spoke his sacred name. "Stormdancer!"

Stormdancer. Her lover wasn't Witchman, after all. She should never have doubted him! Gladly, she flew into his arms, shared emotions if not a more primal embrace.

They had no time.

The being that was Witchman howled in fury. His features pulsed and transformed. Beneath the painted mask, she suddenly recognized the Spanish captain who had thrust his sword through her Comanche lover's heart and, sitting atop his horse, had ridden her into the dust.

"Francisco Castillo!" she shouted in fury.

"Who do you call now? This Francisco will not help you!"

Startled, she realized Witchman did not know his own identity.

"You are Castillo!" Stormdancer cried, hugging Snakewoman close to his side. "Three hundred years ago, you followed me through the secret entrance to this pueblo and massacred the people who lived here!"

Witchman stood still, his body tense with fury. "Enough of your lies!"

"Why do you want to kill again?" Snakewoman asked, clinging to Stormdancer. "Don't you have enough blood and destruction on your conscience?"

Hissing in answer, Witchman threw a stick to the earthen floor and muttered a curse. The stick shape-shifted and slithered toward her. A sidewinder, fangs dripping!

"Spirits guide me!" Stormdancer cried, setting her aside.

He swooped down, grabbed the rattler behind the base of its head and hurled it past Witchman, out of the pueblo ruins and down into the canyon.

Witchman laughed. "You should have thrown it at me. But you are a weak fool! No doubt that's why I killed you before!"

Now he was remembering, she realized. But this man's vision hadn't been called forth for the sake of knowledge. He wanted to destroy them!

Chanting sacred words, she threw her prayer stick directly at Witchman. In awe herself, she stepped back as the carved-wood, feather-decorated prayer stick grew and transformed into a great blue serpent that towered over him.

The eyes of the creature glittered with rainbow colors. It wove a dance and hissed, the sound reverberating through the ancient surroundings.

"Palolokon!" Recognizing the ancient god that slithered closer, Witchman stepped back farther and farther until he was teetering at the edge of the cliff.

Snakewoman knew that with one command, the evil would be dead. But killing and hatred must end or the Kisi would continue to be cursed, if not destroyed completely. She raised her hand and once more cried,

"*Palolokon!*" and the prayer stick returned to her hand.

Stormdancer encircled her waist. Together they had the strength to conquer anyone or anything.

Gazing into Witchman's insane red eyes, she said, "I forgive you for the destruction of my people...for the murder of my lover...for my own death."

Again Witchman's face transformed to that of the Spanish captain, and for a moment his expression altered from hate-filled to peaceful... and then he purposely took that final, deadly step backward.

Shaken, Snakewoman and Stormdancer gazed down into the canyon. Witchman's sidewinder crawled over his still form, his own magic and guilt having turned against him in a final dance with death.

"Mara! Mara, come back," Luke implored until her lids flickered open.

He stroked her hair as gray light crept into the room. Was it dawn already? Her gaze searched Luke's face, as bloody as it had been in her vision. She found one of his wrists, bruised and bloodied, as well.

"What happened to you?"

"Mahooty and Delgado thought locking me in the kiva would keep me off their backs."

"But you escaped."

"With some help from Victor Martinez."

Victor Martinez—the storm-bringer priest and the first victim. "Did we really do it?" she gasped.

He nodded and took the prayer stick from her clutching fingers. After setting it on a nearby table, he scooped her up against him. "Together."

"The evil is finished," Isabel stated.

"Thank God," Onida added, tears sliding down her cheeks. "And you are both safe."

They clung to each other, and as Mara absorbed Luke's very real, very human warmth, she knew she never wanted to be separated from him again.

"Witchman—who was he?" she murmured against his shoulder. "Mahooty?"

"Let's face the bastard together and find out."

Together had such a wonderful ring. Permanent. Could Luke be feeling the same bond she did?

"Um, you might want these," Onida said, sniffling as she offered Mara her own clothes, now clean and dry.

Taking them from Luke's mother, Mara escaped for a moment to the bathroom where she hurriedly changed. Within minutes, she and Luke were on their way to confront Mahooty. Luke told her how he'd been bound and thrown inside the kiva, and how he'd gotten out using Kisi magic through Victor Martinez's guidance.

Ironically, they found the pueblo bully accompanied by Delgado in the middle of the plaza. The two men were staring down at the mouth of the kiva, while several other curious residents looked on.

His back turned to Luke and Mara, Charlie Mahooty kicked the charred cover to the kiva opening and muttered, "What the hell happened here? How did Naha get out?"

Loud enough for all to hear, Luke answered, "With the help of an elder."

Mahooty whipped around, his eyes wide. "A blind old woman set you free?"

"No, the truth and a fireball—the first I ever created. Victor Martinez gave me a few instructions."

Luke's naming the dead man forced a snicker from Delgado. "You been in the sun too long, man." But Mara could tell he was spooked as he moved away.

Luke stepped closer, growling, "What's your excuse? What made the two of you crazy enough to throw me down there in the first place?"

"I don't need an excuse," Mahooty blustered. "I'm the law and you're—"

"Let's see your warrant for his arrest," Mara insisted.

"He arrested Naha?" one of the onlookers murmured. "What for?"

"Thinks he can do anything he wants," another said, louder.

Though Mara despised Mahooty, knew him for the creep he was, she felt no other sense of recognition. He was what he seemed—a bully and nothing more.

He wasn't the one.

"You're not going to mess with me, Mahooty." Luke took a threatening step closer. "Or *your* butt'll be in jail."

"Hey, getting you out of the way wasn't my idea," he protested.

Mara immediately picked up on the implication. "Then there was no warrant for Luke's arrest."

"Somebody paid me to get Naha out of the way," Mahooty admitted. "He's in the clear."

"Who paid you?" Luke pressed. "Whose idea was it?"

Mahooty clenched his jaw as if he wasn't talking. But the moment Luke grabbed his shirtfront, the coward gave in. "All right, all right. Tom Chalas paid me to get you out of the way."

A murmur rippled around them as Mara met Luke's gaze.

"Let's go," he said, taking her arm. "We've found our man."

Glancing back, Mara realized the spectators were following them and waving to others in their yards or on porches to do the same.

"It makes sense," she said as they rushed toward the grocery store. "I should have picked up the clues. Tom Chalas is a sick man whose art speaks *to* war rather than against it." She remembered the slides of the sculptures that revealed his twisted mind. "If only I'd recognized who he really was when I saw his artwork...."

The Spanish captain, Francisco Castillo.

"You could have what?"

"Maybe saved Rebecca."

Luke threw her a disbelieving look. "You didn't even know who you were. You can't blame yourself. And I'm speaking from experience. I've lived with guilt far too long. I finally had to accept that it was actually paint rags that caused the fire in Arizona. I've harbored a lot of anger in my life but I'm neither an arsonist nor a killer."

They flew into the grocery store only to be stopped cold. Empty.

She closed her eyes. Concentrated. "He's here."

"The back room."

They rushed past counters of canned and packaged goods to the door on the opposite end of the store, even as residents of the pueblo trailed through the entrance after them.

In the back room, Chalas was sprawled out on the floor, the top buttons of his shirt undone. As Luke knelt to feel for a pulse, Mara noted something slithering into the shadows of the supply boxes. A snake? Or a sacred spirit?

Moving closer, she recognized the marks at the base of Chalas's neck—two pinpricks like those made by fangs. She checked the shadows to be careful, though she knew in her heart that this snake wouldn't hurt anyone else. If the rattler did appear, was real, she or Luke would pick it up and release the creature into the desert.

Shuffling noises came from behind her as other people crowded the doorway.

"He's still alive."

Even as Luke made the pronouncement, Chalas's eyelids fluttered open. His eyes were glazed over and his breathing was shallow.

"Someone get an antivenin kit," Mara said, fighting her revulsion to the evil she felt filling the room. "Call an ambulance."

"Don't... bother." Eyes hooded, Tom Chalas was staring straight at her. "You won.... Never make it to a hospital...."

Distressed, Mara said, "It didn't have to come to this. Why did you purposely try to destroy your people?"

"My people? Ha! They held me back.... Elders said too weak to be wise or have visions." Chalas's laughter was broken by a cough. "Showed them."

"Your hatred for the Kisi had nothing to do with this life," Luke stated. "It's part of a three-hundred-year-old vendetta. You couldn't let go."

"You have to let go, to forgive yourself," Mara said urgently, afraid he might give up the last of life before he could do so. "Or we'll spend three more centuries playing the tragedy over and over, and you'll never be free."

She realized all three of them had been dealing with guilt through several lifetimes. Guilt that condemned her to being a white woman and her Comanche lover and the Spanish captain to being Kisi.

"Don't want this to go on..." Chalas was saying, a whistling sound punctuating his words.

"Then forgive yourself," she urged.

"Yes, forgive..." The last word he uttered faded into nothing.

And Mara felt the evil lift from the room.

Chalas was dead. She only hoped his soul was finally at rest.

Luke found a blanket and covered the body. Then he put an arm around Mara and led her from the room. Onlookers parted and made way for them. One of the men offered to see to the paramedics when they finally arrived.

Mara allowed herself to be led back to the house as if in a dream. Once there, Luke shared the news with his mother and grandmother. Onida left the room to make some tea.

"He didn't have to die," Mara said, pacing the length of the room. "If only he had seen the truth and asked for forgiveness before it was too late."

"No one person is to blame for anything that happened," Isabel assured her, already looking stronger, more like the fierce woman Mara had first met. "Evil is allowed to exist when all do not work together for balance in the universe. There will be true peace in the world only when everything works in harmony. Light and dark, earth and sky, male and female...." On the last she stood, a knowing smile curving her lips, and moved toward the doorway. "Onida needs me in the kitchen."

Staring after his grandmother, Luke echoed, "Male and female, indeed." And then he turned to Mara. "Do you think we could work together?"

Together. The word thrilled her. She'd been alone for so very long. "Toward peace in the universe?"

"Healing the Kisi would be a good start. Grandmother is the only spiritual leader left, and she may not have long on this earth. Our people need guidance to come back from the curse."

"I wouldn't know where or how to begin."

"We've already begun." He took her in his arms, though he held her at a distance so he could gaze into her eyes. "We could continue together . . . as man and wife."

Her eyes rounded and her heart thrummed. "You want to marry me?"

"I've loved you for more than three hundred years, Mara." His eyes, his voice, held heat. "Isn't it time you finally told me you won't make me wait any longer?"

"Oh God, no longer, please!"

She threw her arms around Luke's neck. In her heart, Mara knew that the guilt of the past was finally vanquished. Their kiss was filled with hope for a lifetime of promise. Together. Always together from now on.

Three hundred years was longer than anyone should have to wait for love.

* * * * *

SILHOUETTE *Shadows*

Welcome To The
Dark Side Of Love...

COMING NEXT MONTH

#56 THE ABANDONED BRIDE—Jane Toombs

Always a Bridesmaid!

Lucy Maguire's prenuptial jitters turned to outright terror when a stranger brought her wedding to a dead stop—and sent her soon-to-be husband fleeing. But what chilled her to the bone was her sensual link to dark knight Max Rider. He claimed Lucy's fiancé was evil incarnate—and that danger had only just begun. Yet Lucy had to wonder if her greatest threat was from Max himself....

COMING IN TWO MONTHS

#57 WOLF IN WAITING—Rebecca Flanders

Heart of the Wolf

She stood between him and an empire. Outcast Victoria St. Clare was a rare beauty, and one of an even rarer breed. Noel Duprey knew that to claim his rightful position of power, he had to expose her for the traitor she was rumored to be. Yet Noel could not control his desire for the one woman capable of determining his fate—and breaking his heart.

It's our 1000th Special Edition and we're celebrating!

Join us these coming months for some wonderful stories in a special celebration of our 1000th book with some of your favorite authors!

Diana Palmer
Debbie Macomber
Phyllis Halldorson

Nora Roberts
Christine Flynn
Lisa Jackson

mini-series by:

Lindsay McKenna, Marie Ferrarella, Sherryl Woods, Gina Ferris Wilkins.

And many more books by special writers.

And as a special bonus, all Silhouette Special Edition titles published during Celebration 1000! Will have **double** Pages & Privileges proofs of purchase!

Silhouette Special Edition...heartwarming stories packed with emotion, just for you! You'll fall in love with our next 1000 special stories!

PRIZE SURPRISE SWEEPSTAKES!

This month's prize:

BEAUTIFUL WEDGWOOD CHINA!

This month, as a special surprise, we're giving away a bone china dinner service for eight by Wedgwood**, one of England's most prestigious manufacturers!

Think how beautiful your table will look, set with lovely Wedgwood china in the casual Countryware pattern! Each five-piece place setting includes dinner plate, salad plate, soup bowl and cup and saucer.

The facing page contains two Entry Coupons (as does every book you received this shipment). Complete and return *all* the entry coupons; **the more times you enter, the better your chances of winning!**

Then keep your fingers crossed, because you'll find out by September 15, 1995 if you're the winner!

Remember: The more times you enter, the better your chances of winning!*